BK#

15

FINAL NOTE

Other books by Dorothy P. O'Neill:

The Liz Rooney Mystery Series

Double Deception
Fatal Purchase
Ultimate Doom
Smoke Cover

Romances by Dorothy P. O'Neill

'L' is for Love
Before Summer's End
Beyond Endearment
Change of Heart
Heart's Choice

FINAL NOTE

•

Dorothy P. O'Neill

AVALON BOOKS
NEW YORK

PRINTED IN THE UNITED STATES OF AMERICA
ON ACID-FREE PAPER
BY HADDON CRAFTSMEN, BLOOMSBURG, PENNSYLVANIA

To My Grandchildren

Braden and Stephanie
Gillian, Brian, Elise, and Anna
Kristen, Lauren, and William

Prologue

In his Manhattan office on Forty-third Street, just off Broadway, talent manager Sid Kohner gnawed at his graying mustache and groped for the pack of Camels in a bulging pocket of his wrinkled jacket. Lighting up, he glared across the desk at his latest discovery. *Discovery?* Hell, what he'd done with Buford Doakes was more like a creation.

From the black Stetson with the diamond-studded band, the custom-tailored Western style pants and jacket down to the hand-crafted boots, the kid had been transformed like a male version of Cinderella. But now he was getting too big for his designer britches. Now he was objecting to one of the places on his forthcoming tour.

Rather than listen to the kid complain, Sid tuned him out and did a little reminiscing. It was barely two years since his car broke down in Gulch City, Texas, while he was on his way from Nashville to an uncle's funeral in Lubbock. It was late afternoon, and the only auto repair shop in town had to send to Amarillo for parts. He had no choice but to spend the night in one of the two local motels.

That evening he dropped into a bar and grill and happened upon a handsome, blond, curly-haired country singer—in his early twenties, Sid had guessed. Even in baggy blue jeans and checkered polyester shirt his rangy form looked good. And the strum of the cheap guitar couldn't keep Sid from recognizing the kid's voice and style as the best he'd heard since Elvis. After too many lean years as agent to country music wannabees who hadn't quite made it, he'd finally struck it lucky.

The cheap guitar was history, of course, along with the discount store clothes. The simple country boy began to disappear during his first tour. Besides his great voice and looks, the kid had a million-dollar smile which he flashed after each song. Those dimples could turn grandmothers into groupies.

Seeing hundreds of adoring faces and outstretched arms and hearing the shrieks and screams, it didn't take Buford long to get the idea that he was God's gift to women.

Having the kid evolve from a nice, simple country boy into a conceited horse's ass was something he could put up with if that's all there was to it, Sid thought. But that was only the beginning. Buford became a full-fledged womanizer. Then he started boozing and smoking pot. Now he was on cocaine. Lecturing him, warning him, got no results. Knowing he was a big moneymaker had given the kid a sense of power.

Lately, Sid had been comparing himself with Dr. Frankenstein.

But whatever control the kid believed he had, it didn't include dictating where he would or would not perform. Bookings for the coming summer would stand firm.

"Buford, shut up and listen to me for a change," Sid said. "I'm telling you, Lorenzo's-on-the-Lake is a top resort—been featuring headliners for sixty, seventy years. It still has a reputation as a real classy place. People stay at the inn for vacations—others drive there from New York and all over just to catch the shows."

Buford pushed his black, diamond-banded Stetson back from his curly, blond bangs. "I never heard of it. Sounds like a hick place to me."

Like the kid wasn't a duded-up hick himself.

"You've hardly ever heard of anyplace but Madison Square Garden and Vegas," Sid growled. "If Lorenzo's was good enough for Eddie Foy Junior and George M. Cohan, it oughta be good enough for you."

Buford looked blank. "Eddie who?"

Suddenly Sid felt old. Showbiz great Eddie Foy Junior was way before the kid's time. Of course he wouldn't know about the legendary vaudeville family show, headed by Eddie's father, Eddie Foy Senior, or that *The Seven Little Foys* was a class act in its day and there'd even been a movie about it, starring Bob Hope.

Buford's voice came into his musings. "And who the hell is George M. Cohan?"

Sid suppressed an exasperated sigh. No use mentioning Jimmy Durante or Bojangles Robinson. The kid probably never heard of *them,* either.

"Well, all right, then, Johnny Cash and Frank Sinatra," he snapped.

At last Buford showed some interest. "Johnny Cash played there, and Sinatra?"

"Sure. All the big names, past and present."

"Elvis?"

"Sure, and Judy Garland and Tammy Wynette." Realizing he should get at least one current female entertainer into the pitch, Sid added, "And Alison Krauss."

Buford looked impressed. "How come they wanted to perform there?"

"Lorenzo Marone was an old timer in show business . . ." Sid began. He stopped short, noticing that Buford had suddenly become aware of the young female office assistant standing on a step stool, reaching for something on a high shelf. Her tight black sweater had parted from her equally tight, short black skirt, revealing her navel and several inches of pink flesh.

Sid knew anything he had to say would be lost in the distraction. No use wasting his breath explaining that Lorenzo Marone was a legend in his own time, a vaudeville song and dance comic so beloved by his peers that when he retired and opened a lakeside inn in the Pocono Mountains, they all rallied to his support, and Lorenzo's-on-the-Lake became famous for its entertainment. Everybody who was anybody in showbiz appeared there over the years, attracting such crowds that Lorenzo had to build a large concert hall and an amphitheater adjacent to the inn.

When Lorenzo died, his sons took over, and now his grandchildren were running the place, but the legend lived on. Current stars who never knew the old vaudevillian clamored to perform where two generations of showbiz greats had appeared before them.

Sid hoped that Buford would behave himself during his weekend booking at Lorenzo's. So far, his image as a wholesome country boy had endured. But incidents involving groupies and drugs had already started some whispers. However, they weren't widespread yet. By the time they were, the kid would be too famous for it to matter. Like others before him, charisma would overshadow character.

He'd go along on the kid's summer tour, Sid decided. That way he could monitor the women invited to the pre-concert bash he'd talked Buford into, replacing the usual after-the-show party. No more underage groupies, spellbound by Buford's performance. No more risk of having him hauled up on charges of corrupting minors. Buford balked at this and threatened to get a new manager. He gave in when Sid told him that mature young women might be as susceptible to his charms as teenagers.

Being divorced had its advantages, Sid thought. He could travel with Buford without complaints from a wife. Unlike the kid's music arranger, whose wife refused to believe it was sometimes necessary for him to go on tour with Buford. She hounded the poor schmo constantly by phone, accusing him of enjoying himself without her. In a contest to choose the typical henpecked husband, Erwin Sporn would win by a landslide. Even before his recent marriage, Erwin was a two-shaves-a-day guy and a lint picker who always dressed nice. But now he was even more so. And from the clothes his wife had him wearing these days, you'd think polyester was poison. Now he was a spotless Dapper Dan—a combination of Mr. Clean and the Brooks Brothers.

Sid's thoughts returned to the argument. "Cut the gripes about Lorenzo's," he said. "You're playing there the last weekend in July. That's final."

Buford looked away from the skin show on the step stool. "From what you said, I guess I can hack it," he replied with a shrug. "But you better round up some frisky little fillies for the party."

Sid held back an exasperated grunt. The kid was obsessed with having good-looking young females all over him. He loved being photographed with as many as his arms and lap would hold, surrounded by them in a hot tub, drinking champagne.

But Sid had heard that Lorenzo's golf and tennis facilities attracted young singles for weekends. He felt confident some unattached women would be there the last weekend in July, young and pretty enough to invite to Buford's party the night before the concert, yet mature enough so there wouldn't be any trouble.

Suddenly Buford broke into a dimpled grin. "Well, I guess that gig's gotta be okay if Elvis played there," he said. "I heard Elvis got lucky everywhere he went. No reason why this Lorenzo place won't be lucky for me, too."

Chapter One

"Well, Sophie, we're on our way," Liz Rooney said, turning her grandmother's 1991 Chevy onto the highway. "Lorenzo's-on-the-Lake, here we come,"

"Yeah—seems like old times," Sophie replied.

During their college years, Liz and best-friend-since-first-grade Sophie Pulaski had taken many a jaunt together. This was the first such trip since Sophie had entered the NYPD Police Academy and met Ralph Perillo. Now Sophie and Ralph were planning an October wedding.

"I'm tickled this worked out," Sophie added. "Me off all weekend and Ralph on duty. That doesn't happen often."

"It was just good luck," Liz replied. This trip was running on good luck all the way, she thought. Gram had taken a chance in a church raffle and won a free weekend for two at a posh Pocono Mountain resort, but she wasn't interested in going.

"What would someone my age do in a place like that all weekend?" she asked. "I'm not into tennis or golf, and I don't even own a swimsuit."

"There's always some top entertainer there every Saturday night," Liz said. "You should go, Gram. Ask one of your church friends to go along."

Gram shook her head. "I want *you* to go, instead. Get Sophie to go with you. You two haven't been on a trip together for a long time."

There'd been many changes during that time, Liz reflected. After college, Pop's close friend, Medical Examiner Dan Switzer, gave her a clerical job in his office that tied right in with her passion for following and trying to solve murder cases. Then, when Pop retired as a detective with NYPD Homicide, he and Mom moved from Staten Island to Florida, and she moved into a one-room apartment in Manhattan. She had no need for the Mustang she'd been given when she graduated from high school. Pop insisted she sell it and use the money to fly down and visit them often.

"I'd love to take you up on the offer, Gram," she said, "but how would we get there? You know I don't have my car anymore."

"Take my car," Gram replied. "It's old but it will get you there and back."

Liz knew it would. The old Chevy had been Grandpa's pride and joy. He'd taken excellent care of it, and after he died Gram continued treating it like it was a Rolls Royce. It had fewer than thirty thousand miles on it.

"Oh, thanks, that would be great, Gram," she said. "I don't know if Sophie will want to spend a whole weekend away from Ralph, but I'll try and persuade her."

It all fell into place. And to top it off, they'd found out that country rock star Buford Doakes would be appearing at Lorenzo's on the weekend they'd chosen. Neither of them was a rabid Buford fan, but it would be fun to see and hear him live.

Sophie's voice came into her thoughts "What did Ike say when you told him we were going to be a couple of Buford Doakes groupies this weekend?"

"What could he say except he hoped we enjoy ourselves?" Liz replied. Unlike Sophie and Ralph, her relationship with NYPD Homicide Detective Ike Eichle hadn't reached the engagement stage. Ike wasn't what you'd call a fast worker. Recently, after more than five months of dating, he finally told her he loved her. Five months was long enough for her to know she wanted to be Ike's wife. But, even though she let him know she loved him too, she wasn't counting on him mentioning marriage anytime soon. Maybe this was just what Ike needed. Maybe not seeing her for an entire weekend would jolt him into popping the question. If he did, she hoped she could restrain herself from saying yes even before the words were out of his mouth.

As they headed north toward the Poconos, she noticed the traffic was light for a Friday evening. She commented on this, adding, "We'll make good time."

"Let me know when you want me to drive awhile," Sophie replied.

"Oh, we'll be there before I need a break. I'm so used to this car, it's like being in an easy chair. You remember I learned to drive in this old buggy when it was new. Even though I aced Driver's Ed, Mom and Gram insisted on coaching me anyway."

Sophie laughed. "How could I forget? They had you driving all over Staten Island, making sure you got used to the one way streets, especially in New Dorp."

The toot of a car horn sounded from behind them. Liz checked the rearview mirror. "What's that all about?" she asked. "I'm going the speed limit and that driver has plenty of room to pass us."

Sophie glanced over her shoulder. "It's those guys in the Lexus we passed a few miles back," she said. "Looks like they want to play a little highway footsie with the red-headed babe behind the wheel."

Liz laughed. "And the cute blond chick in the passenger seat."

Sophie gave the Lexus another look. "There's a bunch of guys in the car," she said. "From what I can see, they're young—maybe high school or college kids."

"Times have changed," Liz said. "The guys we hung around with at that age wouldn't be driving around in a Lexus."

Just as she spoke, the Lexus shot past them. The driver eased it into a space just ahead of them and slowed down.

"I know how this works," Sophie said. "Now *we're* supposed to pass *them*."

"I'll pass them, all right," Liz said, "but I'll drive into that rest area just ahead."

"Don't do that," Sophie said. "They'll think we want them to follow us in. Just keep behind them and don't pass them again. They'll get tired of driving slowly and we'll be rid of them." She looked at Liz with a grin. "Not so long ago we'd have gone along with this foolishness."

"Amazing what a few years will do," Liz replied. A sudden thought struck her. "Buford Doakes is very popular with high school and college kids. What if those boys are on their way to Lorenzo's, too?"

"The place will be packed with young, female Buford fans," Sophie replied. "Those Lexus guys would be like kids in a candy shop. They wouldn't bother with two mature young women." She wiggled her hand. "Especially when one of them is wearing an engagement ring."

"Too bad I don't have one, too," Liz said. "Maybe I should have picked up a fake diamond ring to wear this weekend."

Sophie gave her a teasing glance. "You'll be wearing the real thing soon."

"*Soon!* Are you kidding?" Liz retorted. "You remember how long it took Ike to decide he even wanted to be friends with me."

"That was because he still saw you as Homicide Detective Frank Rooney's daughter with a passion for following murder cases . . ." Sophie began.

"And you know what a pain he was about *that*," Liz said. Vivid recollections of Ike's hostility sprang into her mind. He was especially hostile when she showed up at crime scenes with her boss, the medical examiner. She didn't believe he'd ever want to be friends. Sophie knew all about this. Ike's query, "What are you doing here, Rooney?" had become a buzz-phrase, and Detective Sourpuss their special name for him.

Sophie laughed. "But Detective Sourpuss sweetened up after you stumbled onto that hot clue in the Ormsby murder case."

Remembering, Liz smiled. She and Ike became friends after that. But when their friendship progressed to something more, it was a long, frustrating wait before he got around to mentioning love.

She'd wanted Ike to be the one to broach the subject of love. She'd dropped hints almost to the point where she was mentioning it herself. Sophie knew all about this, too.

She glanced at Sophie with a wry smile. "And you're telling me I'll be wearing an engagement ring soon?" she asked. "Much as I'd like being swept off my feet, I've gotten used to Ike dragging *his*."

As she spoke, they saw the Lexus pull away from its place just in front them and roar off. Seconds later it was out of sight.

"I knew they'd get tired of waiting for us to pass them again," Sophie said. "I'm glad that's over with."

Liz nodded. "If they are on their way to hear Buford Doakes, they'll get there way ahead of us, and we won't meet them in the parking area."

"This must be Stroutsboro," Sophie said, as they drove through a bustling town. "Only about fifteen miles to go. The next town is Bucksville. It's very small—I could hardly find it on the map. When we get there we'll be just a few minutes from the lake."

A scant half hour later, they rounded the crest of a hilly road and saw the lake in the distance below—blue water shot with golden rays of the setting sun. Beyond a grove of tall pines, a large, rambling, white structure nestled at the water's edge. Except for what appeared to be a recently added top floor, its architecture harked back to the days of gables, cupolas and verandahs.

"Lorenzo's-on-the-Lake," Liz murmured. "Just think of all the famous entertainers who've played here."

"And tomorrow night Buford Doakes will be added to the list," Sophie replied.

"That other building must be the concert hall," Liz said, pointing to a structure nearby. "And look, there's an amphitheater, too."

They followed the winding road down the green-shaded slope, through stands of pines and oaks. They glimpsed tennis courts and the first tee of a golf course. They crossed a bridge spanning a brook rushing its way toward the lake.

"I see a path along the brookside and up the hill," Sophie said. "Good thing we brought our hiking boots. We can get in some serious walking while we're here."

Moments later they came to the parking area. Liz steered the Chevy through stone gateposts. As they pulled into a spot not far from an entrance, they saw a huge swimming pool beyond a stone wall.

"Why would they have a swimming pool with that beautiful lake right here?" Sophie asked as they got out of the car.

"I guess they had to keep up with the times," Liz replied. "They probably have hot tubs in the rooms, too."

Sophie laughed. "You can bet we won't have a hot tub in our weekend freebie, but the expensive digs probably have them—like that top floor we saw. They probably call it the penthouse suite. Most likely that's where Buford Doakes will be staying."

"I've heard he seldom takes off his black cowboy hat with the diamond band," Liz said, unlocking the trunk. "I wonder if he keeps it on when he's in a hot tub."

The mental picture of Buford Doakes in a hot tub, wearing his diamond-studded black Stetson, made them both laugh.

"I'll bet he keeps it on," Sophie said. "According to everything I've read about him, he never lets that hat out of his sight. He doesn't want to take a chance on somebody swiping the band off it. Those diamonds are real."

"How much of that is true and how much is publicity?" Liz asked as they took their luggage out of the trunk. "Maybe they're fake diamonds and it's just a gimmick."

"Maybe, but nobody better try and steal that hatband while NYPD officer Sophie Pulaski is on the premises," Sophie said with a grin.

"I hope you're not going to flash your badge around," Liz said. "This is supposed to be a fun weekend."

"Don't worry, I'll keep my badge out of sight, and my gun, too," Sophie replied.

At that moment they heard a voice behind them. "Allo, señoritas."

They turned to see a young, Hispanic-looking man wearing a Lorenzo's-on-the-Lake ID on his jacket, and the embroidered name, *Pedro*. "You need help?" he asked. "I got cart for your bags."

This weekend wasn't costing them a dime and they could afford to splurge on tips, Liz decided. She shot a questioning glance at Sophie, who nodded.

"Yes, thank you, Pedro," Liz replied. "We've never been here before and we don't know where the registration desk is, or anything."

Pedro was already loading their bags onto the luggage cart. "Follow me," he said. "I take care of everything for you."

He led the way across the parking area to the entrance. They were about halfway there when Sophie nudged Liz's arm and gestured toward a nearby car.

"Isn't that the same Lexus we saw on the road?"

Liz sized up the car. "It has a New Jersey plate and it looks like it. Oh, well, like you said, those boys aren't going to come on to us. Tomorrow there'll be dozens of teenaged girls swarming in for the concert."

Pedro must have overheard them. He flashed a grin at them over his shoulder. "Plenty girls coming here for concert tomorrow night. Some here already."

"I guess Buford Doakes won't be here till tomorrow," Liz said.

"He already come today with all his people," Pedro replied. "He have party in his rooms tonight."

He must have quite an entourage, Liz thought. Most big entertainers did. Backup musicians, bodyguards, companions, spouses, photographers . . .

"Have you seen Buford Doakes up close, Pedro?" Liz asked as they walked toward the entrance.

"Sure," he replied. "I help him and all his people with bags."

Inside, he pointed out the registration desk. "I wait for you by elevator," he said.

Only a few people were in the lobby. A middle-aged couple sat on a couch, talking. Several inn guests clustered around an exhibit of photographs near the registration desk. Four young women, wearing shorts and carrying tennis racquets, stood waiting for an elevator. Two men were standing nearby. One of them, balding, with a droopy gray mustache, and wearing a rumpled shirt and pants that looked like he'd slept in them, eyed the tennis players up and down. When he noticed Liz and Sophie, he gave *them* a thorough once-over, too.

The other man, younger, meticulously groomed and fashionably dressed in tan flannel slacks, crisp white cotton shirt and carefully draped paisley patterned cravat, looked like a character in an old British movie. His full head of light brown hair, sprinkled with gray, was combed into a perfect side part. A good-looking man for his age, Liz thought, which she judged to be about fifty. He was deep in conversation on his cell phone and, unlike his untidy, ogling companion, he didn't even glance at them.

"Get that old man with the gray mustache giving us the eye," she said.

"If it isn't teenaged boys it's senior males," Sophie replied.

Evidently Pedro overheard their comments. "That old man, he manager for Buford Doakes. The other one, he with Buford, too. I find out he work on the concert music."

Liz made a mental note to consult Pedro if they should ever want information about Buford Doakes and his entourage, or anyone else at the inn, for that matter.

She was surprised there weren't more people in the lobby. "Where are all the groupies Pedro told us were here already, and where are the Lexus kids?" she asked, as she and Sophie went to the registration desk.

Sophie checked her watch. "In the dining room. I guess— or maybe the girls are in their rooms, primping for Buford's party tonight."

Liz nodded. She'd read enough about Buford Doakes to know when he was on tour he regularly invited young female fans to party with him.

"It will be interesting to see what our freebie room's like," Sophie said, after they checked in. "I hope we haven't been put in a remodeled broom closet."

"You can bet we haven't been given the Presidential Suite," Liz replied, "but no matter where they put us, we'll be eating the same food as people in the deluxe accommodations."

"Food . . ." Sophie said. "I'm starved."

"Me, too," Liz replied. Both she and Sophie had healthy appetites, but Sophie's was bigger. So was her dress size, a ten to Liz's six.

"Let's find Pedro and go up to our broom closet," Sophie said. "We need to change out of our shorts, so we won't be ogled in the dining room."

Chapter Two

T heir room was on the second floor. As they expected, it wasn't spacious and it didn't have a hot tub or a view of the lake. But, as Sophie pointed out, a small room overlooking the parking lot was okay when the price was right.

"I told Ralph I'd phone him to let him know we got here okay," Sophie said, taking her cell phone out of her purse. "I guess you want to call Ike."

Liz nodded. Ike had asked her to phone him when they arrived at Lorenzo's. "I want to be sure you got there without any incidents," he'd added with a grin—a teasing reference to the predicaments she managed to get herself into. She had to admit she'd been in some scary situations, like being held against her will in the apartment of a deranged woman and being kidnapped by two Russian Mafia underlings. But that sort of thing only happened during her amateur sleuthing. She'd reminded him that this wasn't going to be a snooping weekend.

While Sophie talked to Ralph, Liz picked up the room phone to call Ike. She'd forgotten to bring her cell phone, but she didn't need it anyway—Sophie had hers.

Ike answered on the second ring. "Liz?"

The sound of his voice quickened her heart. In her mind she could see his gray eyes and rugged features, and the unruly thatch of sandy hair that gave him a somewhat boyish look. The old saying, don't judge a book by its cover, fit Homicide Detective Ike Eichle perfectly. There was nothing boyish about the way he zeroed in on his cases. Pop often said Ike was the best young detective he'd ever worked with.

"We got here a few minutes ago," she replied. "It was an easy drive."

"Have you seen the big star yet?"

"No, but we were told he arrived this afternoon. The concert's tomorrow night, but some of his fans are here already, and we heard he's throwing a party in his suite tonight."

Ike was silent for a moment before asking, "You going?"

"Of course. We got an engraved invitation." She laughed. "Seriously, I think the party's for the people Buford brought with him and maybe some groupies. Besides, he doesn't even know we're here."

"Let's hope you can keep it that way," Ike teased. He paused. "I miss you, Liz."

"I miss you, too." Right about now, they'd be having dinner at her apartment.

"You'll be back Sunday night?"

"Yes. I'll call you."

"Say hello to Sophie for me. I hope you enjoy yourselves up there."

"We will. It's beautiful here, and there's so much to do."

"I know it's a beautiful area. My grandparents had a farm near Bucksville, a few miles from that lake. I used to spend summers there when I was a kid."

They said good-bye. A few minutes later Sophie ended her call to Ralph. Liz and Sophie changed out of their shorts and tees to outfits more appropriate for the dining room of the posh resort.

"Nobody would ever take you for a cop," Liz said, eyeing Sophie's cornflower blue shirt and slacks and her blond hair swinging loose from its NYPD updo. "In that outfit, you look like a Hollywood star."

"And nobody would ever take *you* for an amateur homicide snoop," Sophie replied. "That green pants outfit goes great with your eyes and hair. It makes you look like a fashion model."

Liz laughed, "Now that we've bolstered up each other's egos, let's go get some dinner."

When they got off the elevator they noticed an oversized photo of Buford Doakes on an easel. He was wearing his trademark black Stetson with the diamond-studded band and holding a fancy guitar. Large lettering appeared below the photo.

PERFORMING SATURDAY NIGHT

"You gotta admit, he's cute," Sophie said.

Just as she spoke, Liz saw the same two men they'd noticed earlier. Again, the one with the gray mustache and the wrinkled clothes looked them over, head to toe. Again, the neatly dressed one with the cravat was too busy talking on his cell phone to notice them. He seemed troubled, she thought, as if he were being harassed.

At that moment, a bevy of giggling girls coming out of the dining room diverted the elder man's attention. The average age of the group appeared to be sixteen, Liz judged. They were dressed in the latest teen craze, most featuring navels, some jeweled.

"Our mothers wouldn't have allowed us out of the house in get-ups like that," Liz said, as she and Sophie headed for the dining room.

"And they'd never have let us go off for a weekend on our own, at that age," Sophie added. "I guess modern parents think there's safety in numbers, and if they go in a bunch, it's okay."

Liz glanced over her shoulder with a frown. "I hope you're right. Look, now that man with the gray mustache is sizing up those young girls."

The dining room was almost full. Couples or quartettes of varying ages occupied most of the tables, Liz noticed, but at a table in the center of the room, she saw a large group of men. Two had long hair, suggesting they might be musicians. She got the feeling they all might be part of Buford's entourage.

Sophie must have had the same thought. "I guess Buford's having room service in his suite to avoid being mobbed by the groupies," she said.

As a waitress led them across the dining room, they passed four young men at a corner table.

Sophie lowered her voice. "There they are—our Lexus Lotharios. Now that I have a good look at them, they're older than I thought."

Liz took a quick glance and had to agree. "Right," she whispered. "They're around our age. Isn't that a little too mature to be interested in teenaged Buford fans?"

"Yeah, like Mr. Mustache in the lobby," Sophie replied.

The waitress seated them at a table beside a window from which they could see the lake, now reflecting the sky's crimson, gold and blue.

"Red sky at night, sailor's delight," Liz said. "Looks like tomorrow's going to be a beautiful day."

"Let's get up early and hike the trail along the brook," Sophie suggested. "Then after lunch we can go for a swim. What'll it be, the lake or the pool?"

Liz glanced out the window. "I'd like to try the lake. It'll probably be cold, though. Remember the lake at Girl Scout camp?"

Sophie laughed. "Yeah. 'Bracing,' the swimming counselor called it. But I'm with you. I'd like to try the lake. If it's too cold we can go to the pool."

The waitress came to take their orders. The menu offered a varied selection, including a number of Italian dishes. They both ordered cannellonis and salads.

"We should have Italian wine, too," Sophie said, picking up the wine list.

The waitress smiled. "I was just going to tell you, the gentlemen at the corner table want to buy you each a glass of wine."

Liz and Sophie both turned their heads to look at the Lexus quartette. Not surprising, all four were looking at them, smiling.

"Should we?" Liz asked. "Letting them buy us drinks might give them expectations."

"They look like okay guys. I think they're just being friendly," Sophie replied. "Besides, if they had ulterior motives they'd hit on a table of *four* women."

Liz hesitated, then shrugged. "All right."

They smiled and nodded at the four men, and ordered glasses of Chianti. A few minutes later, they were raising their goblets in unison with the corner quartette.

"I know what happens next," Sophie said. "When they finish eating they'll stop by our table."

About twenty minutes or so later, Liz grinned at Sophie. "You're fairly accurate. One of those guys is headed this way. The others are hanging back, like they want him to break the ice."

The approaching young man had reddish hair and a nice, slightly freckled face. When he reached their table, they both looked up at him smiling.

"Thanks for the wine," Liz said.

He returned the smile. "Our pleasure. We thought we should do something to make up for our antics on the road today. We were just having a little fun. I hope we weren't too annoying."

"It's okay," Liz said.

Sophie nodded in agreement.

"My name is Walt Halloran," the young man said. He paused, waiting for them to introduce themselves.

"I'm Liz Rooney," Liz said.

With her left hand, Sophie brushed an imaginary tendril of hair away from her face, slowly, to make sure he couldn't miss her engagement ring. "And I'm Sophie Pulaski," she said. "I guess you and your friends are here for the concert tomorrow night."

Walt shook his head. "This is a golf weekend for us. We didn't plan it around the concert. We didn't know about the Buford concert till we got here."

"You mean you're not going to the concert?" Sophie asked.

"Oh, since we're here we couldn't pass up a chance to hear Buford Doakes in person," Walt replied. "We're all going except Larry. He doesn't—"

At that moment the other three converged on the table. Walt introduced them. Dennis, a chubby towhead, Jim, tall, with brown hair, and dark-haired Larry. Liz took special notice of Larry, wondering why this good-looking young man wasn't going to the concert tomorrow night.

Evidently Walt had been appointed spokesman for the group. "We were hoping you'd join us in the lounge after you finish dinner," he said. "There's a piano player who is supposed to be great. And dancing. You probably saw the piano player's photo in the lobby."

"No, we didn't," Liz replied. "I guess we were distracted by the photo of Buford." And the gray mustached man ogling them, she thought. She cast a questioning glance at Sophie.

"Sounds like fun," Sophie said, again bringing her left hand into play.

"Great," the group chorused.

"We'll get a table in the lounge and meet you there," Walt said.

Watching the four of them leave the dining room, Liz noticed the occupants of the center table had departed. If they were members of Buford's entourage, they'd gone to join Buford for the party Pedro, the bellman, had mentioned, she decided.

At another table, she noticed the group of four young women tennis players they'd seen in the lobby, earlier. They must have come into the dining room while she and Sophie were occupied with dinner.

"Those gals look like they're around our age," she said.

"Yeah, they do," Sophie replied. "If the Lexus guys were hoping their offer of drinks would lead to pairing off, wouldn't they have invited those four to meet them in the lounge, instead of us?"

Liz nodded. "I guess Walt meant it when he said they came up here especially for golf."

Just as she was thinking she didn't want to spend all evening in the lounge with Walt and his friends, Sophie spoke up. "An hour or so with those guys ought to be enough."

"My thoughts, exactly," Liz replied. "This place has a fascinating history. I'd like to learn more about it, and read about the celebrities who stayed here over the years. There should be books or pamphlets in the lobby, and old photographs or postcards."

"Okay, after we leave our boys in the lounge, let's get some literature and take it to our room," Sophie said.

When they entered the lounge, the piano player was just finishing a rendition of Buford's latest hit song, "True Blue Texas Love." It was quite good, Liz thought. According to news reports, he'd written it himself, lyrics and all, and it was already at the top of the charts.

They spotted Walt and the others at a big table near the piano. All four stood up as they approached. Liz found herself being seated between Walt and Dennis. Sophie was across from her, between Jim and Larry. Liz noticed empty brandy glasses on the table.

"We've already had a round of cognacs and we're about to order seconds," Walt said. "What would you like?"

"Cognac's fine with me," Liz replied.

Sophie nodded. "Fine."

Their brandies were served just as the piano player announced he would play requests. Right away, an elderly couple at a table for two requested "Smoke Gets in Your Eyes."

"That's a real oldie. It must be their special song," Liz said.

"Maybe it's a song they danced to the night they got engaged," Walt said. "And speaking of that—I noticed Sophie's wearing an engagement ring, but you're not. Are you dating anyone seriously?"

"Yes, I am," Liz replied. *How would Ike have answered that question?*

Walt gave a rueful smile. "I should have known."

They started talking. He told her he and the other three had been friends since college. They all worked for firms in southern New Jersey. Every few weeks they got together for golf at some good course.

Liz glanced around the table. Dennis, seated next to her, was talking and laughing with Jim and Sophie. The handsome, dark-haired one, Larry, was silently sipping his brandy.

She recalled what Walt had said, earlier. They were all going to the concert tomorrow night except Larry. He'd started to tell her why when the others had joined them. Now, she was curious.

She lowered her voice. "Why isn't Larry going to the concert?" she asked.

Walt replied, almost in a whisper. "He doesn't like Buford Doakes."

"Well, not everybody enjoys country rock," Liz replied.

"It's not the music," Walt said. He leaned closer to her and spoke softly into her ear. "It's Buford himself. Larry hates his guts."

Jim's voice penetrated her startled reaction. "Liz, Sophie just told me about your grandmother winning the church raffle."

She nodded. "That's right. We're here on a freebie weekend. Everything included—even the concert tomorrow night."

As Liz spoke, she glanced at Larry. The expression on his face seemed to say he'd never attend a Buford Doakes concert, free or not.

Larry must have had a bad experience with Buford, she thought. Her imagination took over. Maybe Larry was from Texas, too, and they'd known one another before Buford became a celebrity, and Larry was harboring an old grudge. Maybe it had something to do with a girl. Had Buford stolen Larry's high school sweetheart? She decided Larry would have gotten over that, long ago. It had to be something more serious and perhaps more recent.

The piano player swung into "The Yellow Rose of Texas"—another tribute to Buford, Liz thought.

"Would you like to dance?" Walt asked.

"I'd love to," she replied. She'd ask him about Larry while they were dancing.

On the dance floor, she changed her mind. Getting Walt to tell her why Larry hated Buford might be asking him to betray a confidence. It didn't matter, anyway. She shouldn't be so curious.

She and Sophie took turns dancing with all four of them. When it was her turn with Larry, she noticed he was very quiet. Was he thinking about Buford? Her curiosity again, she thought. Ike once told her she had the curiosity of a dozen cats.

When the piano player took a break, and they were all back at the table, she caught Sophie's glance. "Have we had enough of this?" it seemed to ask.

She replied with a slight nod. Getting to her feet, she said, "This has been great fun, guys, but Sophie and I are going hiking early tomorrow morning and . . ."

A murmur of protest arose.

"It's so early," Walt said, checking his watch.

"Maybe we'll see you around, tomorrow," Liz said, as she and Sophie left the table.

In the lobby, as planned, they picked up some pamphlets and postcards about the history of Lorenzo's-on-the-Lake. They were on their way to the elevator when they saw the man who'd stared at them earlier, and his companion, who as usual, was talking on his cell phone. The one with the gray mustache started walking toward them, smiling. The other man lagged behind, still talking on the phone.

"Looks like they're coming over to speak to us," Sophie whispered.

A moment later the two men were at their side. Up close, Gray Mustache's clothes looked even more wrinkled, Liz noticed. His pants pockets sagged as if they contained a lot of stuff. She couldn't help noticing the contrast between his slovenly appearance and his companion's impeccably neat look.

Gray Mustache reached into one of his bulging pockets and took out two business cards. While doing this, he also scooped out several wadded-up gum wrappers and a battered cigarette pack, which fell to the floor. He picked up the cigarettes but ignored the gum wrappers. This man was a slob, she thought.

They barely had time to glance at the cards before he spoke. "Allow me to introduce myself and my associate," he said. "I'm Sidney Kohner, Buford Doakes' manager." He inclined his head toward the other man, who'd clicked off his phone but still looked harassed. "And Erwin Sporn, Buford's music arranger."

Liz exchanged a puzzled glance with Sophie. What was this all about?

An instant later, puzzlement changed to surprise as Gray Mustache spoke on. "Buford would be pleased if you girls would join him in his penthouse suite for an informal party this evening."

Chapter Three

It was as if she and Sophie had been stricken mute, Liz thought. They looked at each other, she hoping Sophie would come up with some sort of reply, and Sophie apparently wishing the same about her.

"You can go up to the penthouse any time, now," Buford's rumpled, gray-mustached manager continued. He pointed across the lobby. "There's a private elevator. Show the guard my cards and he'll let you on. Be sure and bring along your bikinis. You'll need to change into them during the evening. There'll be a photo session with Buford in the hot tub."

With that, he and Buford's music arranger turned and walked off.

Sophie glared after them. "The nerve of that guy, taking it for granted we'd jump at the chance to have a hot tub party with Buford. Why didn't you say something?"

"I didn't know what to say. Why didn't *you* say something?"

They both laughed.

"I have to admit I was torn between wanting to tell him to get lost and thinking it might be fun to go to the party," Sophie said.

"Me too," Liz replied. "But of course it's out of the question."

"Yeah. *Bring your bikinis.* Can you imagine us in a hot tub with Buford?"

"And having our photos taken? And having them appear in some tabloid?"

Sophie grinned, "That would go over big with Ralph and Ike."

They took the regular elevator to the second floor. Several people got on with them, so they didn't discuss the incident further till they were in their room.

"An invitation to a big country music star's party," Liz said. "This will be something interesting to tell our grandchildren."

Sophie looked thoughtful. "Yeah, but not as interesting as if we really went."

"Are you suggesting we should go?"

"We could put in an appearance and leave when we feel like it," Sophie said.

"And we wouldn't have to take our bikinis," Liz added.

A look passed between them—the same look they'd been sharing since they were six years old. Its meaning was as clear now as it had been when they were contemplating some childhood mischief or adolescent caper.

Let's do it!

At the private penthouse elevator, they presented Gray Mustache's cards to a shaven-headed guard who was built like a Hummer. Shaven Head studied each card carefully before waving them into the empty elevator.

"For a second I thought he was going to ask us to present our bikinis, too," Sophie said.

When they stepped off the elevator into the foyer of the penthouse suite, they could hear the strumming of a guitar and the unmistakable voice of Buford Doakes singing "True Blue Texas Love." Liz decided she liked Buford's signature song better each time she heard it. Both music and lyrics contained a surprisingly sweet quality. There was no doubt that Buford was as good at composing songs as he was at singing them.

Another burly young man, this one with shoulder-length dark hair and wearing blue jeans and cowboy boots, approached them. Liz recognized him from the dining room. Most likely he and the man at the elevator were Buford's bodyguards who protected him from crazed young fans trying to cut off locks of his hair, she decided.

Cowboy Boots gestured toward an open door. "Go right in girls. Join the party."

They stepped into a spacious room, furnished with plush carpeting, comfortable-looking sofas and chairs and a grand piano. Across the room, Liz saw a hallway—probably leading to the bedrooms, she thought. A wall of windows overlooked the lake, dark, now, but glinting with lights from the inn. On the opposite wall stood a bar, around which a number of women clustered—about a dozen, Liz judged. She spotted the four tennis players in the crowd, along with other young women, none of whom looked as young as the teenagers she'd seen earlier. She recognized the few men present from the dining room—Buford's people.

In the midst of the gathering, like a monarch holding court, Buford Doakes, wearing his usual designer-styled western suit and black, diamond-banded Stetson, was sitting on a high stool, strumming his guitar, crooning his song.

"Looks like only females were invited," Liz whispered to Sophie. "Isn't that a bit strange?"

"Yeah, strange." Sophie gave a slight frown. "I guess that's the way Buford wants it, and from what we experienced in the lobby, his manager is the recruiter."

Liz glanced around. Near the entrance to the bedroom hallway she glimpsed an oversized hot tub behind a row of large, potted plants. She shifted her glance to the crowd at the bar. The men from Buford's entourage were making sure no woman's glass stayed empty.

"After a few more rounds, Buford will probably make an announcement," she said. She lowered her voice. "'Everybody into bikinis. It's hot tub time.'"

"I want to hang around for that," Sophie said, with a grin.

"Me, too. I'd like to see if he wears his hat in the hot tub."

They were both laughing, when a nearby voice startled them. "What do you want to drink?"

They turned to see a blond young woman, about five feet two, Liz judged, nicely built, but somewhat frail-looking. A pretty face, Liz thought, but she would have been more attractive if her hair wasn't overbleached and frizzy and much too long. Liz wondered where she fit into Buford's entourage.

While waiting for a reply, the woman scrutinized them, especially Sophie. Liz detected a trace of hostility in her eyes.

"I'll have a scotch on the rocks please," Sophie said.

Liz shot her a surprised look. It wasn't like Sophie to order a strong drink after wine with dinner and brandy afterwards. But an expression in Sophie's eyes told her to go along with it.

"I'll have the same."

They watched the young woman go toward the bar. Another inch and her frizzy blond hair would reach her rump, Liz noticed.

"How come you ordered scotch?" she asked Sophie.

"Did you notice the way that babe looked at me," Sophie replied, keeping her voice low. "It was like she knew I was a cop."

"And ordering scotch would make her think you weren't?" Liz asked.

"At least it might make her think I'm not here on a possible bust."

"Since when do people get busted for drinking at a party? Anyway, your NYPD badge wouldn't carry any weight around here."

"Yeah, but if Ms. Frizzy Hair suspects I'm a cop, she probably thinks I'm from the local sheriff's department, or whatever they have in this area."

Even though nobody was close enough to overhear, they were keeping their voices close to a whisper.

"I have a feeling Ms. Frizzy Hair knows this party is going to take off in another direction," Sophie continued. "With enough booze under their belts, some of these women might wind up flying high on something besides booze."

"Maybe we should think about leaving before things get too wild," Liz said.

"Don't you want to stay for the bikini shoot?"

"Yes, but let's be very careful or we might find ourselves right up there with the high fliers," Liz said.

They stopped talking when they saw the woman coming back with their drinks.

After she'd gone, Sophie held her glass at arm's length and wrinkled her nose. "Whew, talk about strong—we could get crocked on the smell alone."

Liz jiggled the ice in her glass. "If we hang onto these drinks, nobody will insist we need refills."

Sophie nodded. "Yeah. We'll keep our eyes open and our glasses full. But we'd better steer clear of Ms. Frizzy Hair— she might notice the ice melting."

Enthusiastic applause broke into their talk. Buford had finished his song. One of his cohorts immediately brought him a drink—not his first of the evening, Liz was sure. He drained his glass in two gulps and demanded another. A lackey sprang to get it for him.

"He's on his way to getting smashed," Liz said, as she and Sophie walked closer to the bar.

"He's not the only one," Sophie replied. "Notice the glazed eyes on those women."

Liz nodded. "The tennis players might not make it to the court tomorrow."

Suddenly Sophie gave her a nudge. "Look who just came in."

Liz turned to see Gray Mustache and the dapper music arranger walking toward them. The music arranger was on his phone again. Gray Mustache, or, according to his card, Sidney Kohner, Buford's manager, gave them a wide smile, revealing a double row of tobacco-stained teeth. "Enjoying the party, girls?"

This was the second time he'd addressed them as girls, Liz thought. If he wanted girls at the party, there were plenty of teenagers around. Why hadn't he invited them?

She glanced at the women crowded around Buford at the bar, and another thought took hold. Before the party ended, some of them might emerge as immature as any hysterical, swooning, Buford groupie.

Sophie made a polite reply to Kohner. "It's a very nice party. Buford just finished singing 'True Blue Texas Love.'"

"That's a wonderful song," Liz chimed in. "Buford is really talented. I heard he wrote the lyrics as well as the music. Is that true?"

"Yes. Many good composers write their own lyrics," Kohner replied. As he spoke, he glanced at the music arranger, who was momentarily off the phone. "Isn't that right, Erwin?"

The music arranger gave a nod. "Yes, that's right."

He seemed somewhat grouchy, Liz thought. She decided the music arranger must have some personal problem. A sick wife or kid, maybe. That's why he was always on the phone, looking troubled.

"At the concert tomorrow night, you'll find out that Erwin is very talented, too," Kohner went on. "His arrangements are tops in country rock."

Liz glanced at Sporn, expecting him to acknowledge the compliment. He didn't. Whatever his personal problem was, it really made him grouchy, she thought.

"We're looking forward to the concert," she said.

"Meanwhile, have a good time tonight," Kohner replied.

As the two men walked away, Liz heard the manager say something. The few words she caught were enough to make her think he might be concerned about Buford's drinking. ". . . get him into the hot tub while he's still able to sit up."

Sophie must have heard this, too. "Sounds like he's worried that Buford might be too out of it for the bikini photo shoot," she said. "They must be planning to use tonight's photos for publicity."

Liz glanced at the bevy of women crowding around Buford. "Why do they think they need more publicity shots? Seems like every magazine you pick up has pictures of Buford surrounded by his groupies."

The instant she spoke, the answer came to her. Evidently Buford's manager didn't want Buford photographed with teenagers anymore. He wanted him to be seen with older fans. That's why he'd invited only mature young women to this party.

She expressed her thought to Sophie.

"I'll bet you're right," Sophie said. "Something must have happened between Buford and a teenaged fan. There hasn't been anything in the news, but of course it would have been hushed up."

The appearance of the petite Ms. Frizzy Hair interrupted their talk. She was carrying a tray of drinks.

"I brought you fresh scotches," she said. Her manner was no friendlier than it had been earlier.

Sophie jumped in with a covering lie. "Oh, thanks, but one of the men already brought us refills."

"Well, I'll set these down on this table here," Ms. Frizzy Hair said. "Drink them when you're done with the others. But don't take too long over them. The camera man's getting ready."

"For the hot tub shoot?" Liz asked.

"Yes. Someone will tell you which bedroom to go into to put on your swim suits." With that, Ms. Frizzy Hair turned abruptly and went back to the bar.

"She's not exactly Miss Congeniality," Liz said. "I'd love to know where she fits into the Buford Doakes picture."

"I've heard he has a girlfriend who travels with the entourage—a hometown sweetheart," Sophie replied.

Liz laughed. "If that one's his girlfriend, it's no wonder she's so sour. It has to be rough, seeing him cavorting with other women." She grinned at Sophie. "Maybe that's why she gave you the evil eye before. She didn't think you were a cop—she just thought you were the best looking woman here and Buford would be sure to single you out in the hot tub."

Just as she spoke, a stir of excited voices caught their attention. While they were talking, Buford must have gone to his bedroom and changed into his swimming trunks. Now he'd emerged, tall, tan and magnificently muscular, his black Stetson with the diamond-studded band pushed back on his curly blond head.

"So, he *does* wear it in the hot tub," Liz said.

They watched him saunter, somewhat unsteadily, around the potted plants to the edge of the tub, followed by two male members of his entourage. They helped him get into the water. He flashed his famous dimpled smile.

"It's mighty lonesome in here," he called. "I sure enough would like some company."

What could only be described as a mad scramble took place as the women rushed to get into their bikinis, almost knocking down a man directing them to the bedrooms.

"You can bet they won't spend much time primping," Sophie said. "They all want to be the first one into the tub with Buford."

"Do you suppose we'll be expelled from the party because we're not participating?" Liz asked.

Sophie was about to reply when they both noticed one of the women tennis players coming their way. "Apparently *she* isn't putting on a bikini, either," Sophie said.

The pretty young woman approaching them had a coffee-with-cream complexion. She walked with the easy grace of a natural athlete. Though she was smiling, Liz detected a troubled look in her dark eyes.

"Hi, I'm Gail Hagen," she said. "I'm glad to see I'm not the only one who's passing up the hot tub session."

"Welcome to the Bikini Boycott, Gail," Sophie replied. "I'm Sophie Pulaski."

"I'm Liz Rooney, and we didn't even bring our bikinis," Liz added.

"I brought mine," Gail said, tapping the purse slung over her shoulder. "But I wasn't here very long before I decided I didn't like the way this party was going. I tried to talk my friends into leaving, but . . ." She shrugged.

"It was the drinks," Liz said. "They were much too strong. They'd mess up anyone's good judgment."

"We didn't drink anything, and it looks like you didn't either," Sophie said.

"One sip was enough for me," Gail replied. "I tried to warn my friends, but they were excited about meeting Buford Doakes. I couldn't get through to them."

A voice from behind them broke into their talk. "You'd better hurry up, or you won't get into the picture," the long-haired guard in the cowboy boots said.

As usual, Sophie had a ready reply. "Oh, we forgot to bring our swim suits."

At that moment, a burst of applause from Buford and his entourage greeted the first bikini-clad woman to appear. Others followed. Soon they were all in the tub with Buford—a tight squeeze, but Buford seemed to relish it. He wasted no time putting his arms around as many as he could reach. Liz saw him plant a kiss on a blond woman snuggled into his left shoulder.

Gail looked grim. "That's one of my friends he's slobbering over."

"This might not last long," Sophie said. "Maybe they'll take a few pictures and then the party will be over."

Liz was sure Sophie didn't believe this, and neither did she.

They watched Ms. Frizzy Hair and two men walk around the sides of the tub dispensing drinks. Ms. Frizzy Hair looked sullen. Liz couldn't help feeling sorry for her. If she was Buford's hometown girlfriend, she must feel humiliated by his antics.

Cameras closed in. Numerous shots were taken. The women took turns being photographed with Buford, but Liz noticed he always grabbed Gail's friend and brought her back next to him.

Evidently Sophie noticed this, too. "Gail, it looks like Buford's taken a special shine to your friend," she said.

Gail gave a nod and a sigh. "I hope this breaks up soon."

But Liz noticed the party showed no signs of winding

down. Instead, the merriment appeared to be escalating. The babble of voices and raucous laughter grew louder.

"Look," Sophie said. "One of the bodyguards is passing around a box of cigarettes. Something tells me they're not Camels."

From the look on Gail's face, she'd picked up on this, too. "I hope my friends aren't too smashed to realize what's happening," she said.

Sophie set her drink down on a nearby table. "What do you say we get out of here?"

"I'm all for that," Liz replied. She glanced at Gail.

Gail shook her head. "I'd like to go with you, but I feel as if I should stay and keep an eye on my friends." She took a long look at the hot tub scene and sighed. "Especially Penny—Buford's really hitting on her."

"I don't like leaving you here," Liz said.

"I don't, either," Sophie added.

"I'll be all right. That longhaired guard with the cowboy boots seems like an okay guy. If things get out of hand with Penny, I think I can count on him to help."

Sophie nodded, "Well, if you're sure . . ."

"I'm sure."

"Good luck," Liz said, as they turned to go to the elevator.

"Thanks for your concern. I'll be fine." A flash of humor came into Gail's dark eyes. "But if you hear talk tomorrow that someone hit Buford over the head with his guitar, you'll know who did it."

Chapter Four

Liz awoke before sunrise the next morning. She and Sophie had gone to bed soon after looking at the literature about the history of Lorenzo's-on-the-Lake. They'd pored over photos of the inn in its early days, and read interesting articles relating to the lake and the surrounding area.

"It says here the lake used to freeze solid from late December till early March, and horse-drawn wagons could cross from one side to the other," Sophie quoted.

"Lucky it did," Liz replied, reading another article. "There was no refrigeration in those days. They chopped blocks of ice from the lake and put them in icehouses to use in summer. See this? It's a picture of one of the icehouses. Some of them are still around here, the article says."

Before they turned out the light, they'd rehashed the party.

"From the way things were going when we left, that bash will be blasting all night," Sophie said.

Now, as the first light streaked through the window, Liz felt wide awake and full of energy. Unlike Buford and his tubful of women, she thought, with a wry smile.

In the other bed, Sophie stirred. "You up already?"

"Not quite. I just opened my eyes a minute ago."

"I guess we're slept out," Sophie said. "What do you say we grab an early breakfast and go for a hike along the brook?"

"Sounds okay to me. Let's see what time the dining room opens." Liz got out of her bed and went to the desk to check the inn's information data. "Oh, not till seven," she said. "We have loads of time to shower and get ready."

She turned away from the desk and looked out the window. "I wish we had a view of the lake . . ." she started to say, when she stopped short.

"Sophie, I think there's a police car in the parking lot!"

"What?" Sophie jumped out of bed and joined her. "It looks like a police car, all right," she said as they stared through the semi-darkness at the white and green vehicle below their window. A moment later, she nodded. "Yes, it is. I can barely make out the insignia on the side."

Liz pictured a raid on Buford's party in the wee hours of the morning. "Do you think somebody tipped off the sheriff about the marijuana in the penthouse?" she asked.

"*Something's* happened, that's for sure," Sophie replied. Suddenly she clutched Liz's arm. "Look—over there. Isn't that an ambulance?"

Liz looked. "It certainly is!"

"Let's get dressed and go down to the lobby right now," Sophie said. "The night clerk will be at the desk. Maybe he can tell us what happened."

When they stepped off the elevator the almost eerily-quiet lobby appeared to be empty—not surprising given the early hour. The only sign of life Liz noticed at first was the clerk at the registration desk. But a moment later she spotted a man standing by the penthouse elevator.

"There's a man over there at the private elevator," she told Sophie. "He's not the guard with the shaved head we saw last night, and I don't remember seeing him at the party."

Sophie took a look. "I never saw him before, either. I'm sure he isn't part of Buford's entourage."

"He's not in uniform, but there's no doubt he's guarding that elevator and keeping an eye on the lobby," Liz said. "Could he be a cop?"

"Yeah, maybe a deputy or whatever they have out here in

the boonies." Sophie glanced toward the registration desk. "Let's ask the night clerk some questions."

Liz thought the middle-aged clerk looked troubled when he saw them approaching. Then he forced a smile and a pleasant spiel. "Good morning, ladies. You're up very early. What can I can do for you?"

"We noticed a police car and an ambulance in the parking lot," she said. "Can you tell us what's going on?"

The troubled look reappeared on the clerk's face. "All I know is someone in the penthouse called the paramedics around four o'clock this morning." He paused.

"And . . . ?" Liz asked.

Sophie couldn't restrain her impatience. "And after they left, the police came?"

"That's right. Sheriff MacDuff got here a couple of hours ago," the clerk replied. "Then the doctor from Stroutsboro and then the ambulance."

Sophie turned away and whispered in Liz's ear. "I'll bet somebody died up there and the doctor from Stroutsboro is the county coroner."

"Sure sounds like it," Liz replied. Her imagination took off. She pictured a drug overdose.

The clerk rambled on, as if he were relieved to be talking to someone about the situation. "Sheriff MacDuff's deputy asked me what time I came on duty and I told him last night at eleven. When I told him my shift was up at seven this morning he said I couldn't go home—state troopers are blocking the entrance at the top of the hill. Only county vehicles can get in or out."

At that moment the door to the penthouse elevator slid open and a tall, heavyset young man stepped off. His tan, broad-brimmed hat and brown uniform emblazoned with patches and a metal star left no doubt that he was the sheriff.

After speaking briefly to the man on guard, he glanced around and saw Liz and Sophie. A look of surprise came to his round, affable face. He walked toward them. "Mornin'," he said. "I didn't expect to see any guests in the lobby this early."

As usual, Sophie didn't hold back. "What happened in the penthouse, Sheriff MacDuff?" she asked. Liz was surprised she hadn't asked, "who died?"

The sheriff hesitated before replying. "Guess I might as well tell you. I'll be making a statement soon, anyway."

Just as he spoke, the elevator doors opened again, and two men maneuvered a gurney into the lobby. The dark plastic-shrouded form strapped onto it could not be mistaken for anything but a corpse.

For a few moments Liz and Sophie viewed the macabre scene in silence, before turning their questioning glances to the sheriff.

"It's Buford Doakes," MacDuff told them. "He was found drowned in the penthouse hot tub. And it wasn't an accident."

Chapter Five

"A homicide!" Liz exclaimed, her eyes widening in disbelief.

"Yup, no doubt about it," the sheriff replied. "There was evidence of a struggle. The victim's hat was in the water across from where the body was found and one of the potted plants had been knocked over and set to rights. The pot must have rolled some when it hit the floor. We found it standing a ways apart from the others."

Police procedure must be different in rural areas, Liz thought. She couldn't imagine a big city lawman giving out such detailed information to two total strangers.

It sounded as if Buford or his killer had picked up the toppled plant. It seemed strange that either one would stop to do that, during the fight or afterwards. She turned her thoughts to Buford's Stetson. It must have been knocked off during the fracas and landed in the water. But when she and Sophie left the party, Buford wasn't in top fighting form. He could easily have been pushed into the tub by the person he was struggling with, she decided.

While she tried to recall if there'd been any hint of animosity toward Buford by anyone at the party, the sheriff leveled penetrating looks at each of them.

"Were you ladies at that party last night?"

"Yes, we were," Liz replied.

"I'm going to interview everyone who was on the premises last night, starting with those who were at the party," he said. "I might as well begin with you. First, I'd like to see some ID."

Sophie flashed her NYPD credentials.

MacDuff eyed Sophie with sudden warmth. "So you're a cop, too. A detective?"

"Not yet, but I'm going to apply for training when I'm eligible," Sophie replied.

The sheriff turned to Liz, who'd been about to show him her driver's license. "You an officer too?"

"No," Liz replied, wishing she were.

"But her father's a retired NYPD homicide detective," Sophie added.

"Too bad you two aren't detectives," MacDuff said. "I've had training, but I could use some help. Guess I'll have to send for a detective from the Stroutsboro Police Department." He smiled. "I don't have to spend much time interviewing you two. Just a couple of questions. First, what time did you leave the party?"

"Ten thirty-five," Sophie replied, promptly. "That's accurate. I checked my watch."

MacDuff jotted this down in a notebook. "And while you were there, did you notice anything unusual?" he asked.

"The whole party was unusual," Liz said. "That's why we left."

His wry smile told her he understood exactly what she meant. "Okay," he said. "I'll get back to you if I need to interview you again. But you don't have to hang around indoors. Go ahead with whatever recreational plans you had."

"I guess you're confining everyone to inn property," Sophie said.

"Yup, I just put out the word. State troopers are blocking the road to the entrance till after everyone's been interviewed."

Whoever killed Buford could have fled and might be miles away from the inn by now, Liz thought. But, maybe not. The killer might have figured a missing inn guest would immediately become the prime suspect. Most likely whoever did it was still on the premises. The sheriff probably thought so, too.

"Well, I've got to get back upstairs," MacDuff said. "Thanks for your cooperation." He turned and headed for the penthouse elevator.

"He seems like a nice guy," Liz said.

"Yeah," Sophie replied. "And he seems to know what he's doing. This case is too much for a country sheriff to handle alone. Good thing he's sending for help."

They decided to go to their room and get ready for their hike. By the time they changed out of their hastily-donned clothes, showered, and got into shorts, tee shirts and boots and packed a few trail necessities into their backpacks, the dining room would probably be open. They could have breakfast and then start right out.

On their way across the lobby to the elevator, they noticed the picture of Buford was gone from the easel. "There's some sort of notice there, instead," Liz said.

They walked over to the easel to read what appeared to be a hastily lettered sign.

The Management Regrets That Due to
Unforeseen Circumstances Tonight's
Buford Doakes Concert Has Been Cancelled

"Wow," Sophie said. "That's going to stir up a mess of rumors before MacDuff gets around to making a statement."

They'd almost finished breakfast and had just asked the waitress for bottles of water to take on their hike, when they saw the Lexus quartette come into the dining room. They looked as if they were dressed for a round of golf.

"I wonder if those guys know what happened to Buford," Liz said.

"You can bet they've heard *something*," Sophie replied. "By this time rumors are probably flying all over the inn."

At that moment Walt saw them. He walked over to the table. Jim, Larry and Dennis followed.

Walt looked grim. "Did you hear what we heard, about Buford?" he asked.

"Yes, we did," Liz replied. "We talked with the sheriff a little while ago."

The others crowded around the table, expressing disbelief.

"Buford drowned in the hot tub? Could that be true?" Dennis asked.

"Maybe not," Jim replied. "Maybe the concert was cancelled because he's not feeling well. There's been no official statement. All we heard were rumors."

Walt nodded. "Yeah, there are some pretty wild rumors going around. We even heard the drowning wasn't accidental."

"You say you talked with the sheriff," Jim said. "Is it true the local police are calling this a homicide?"

"Yes," Liz replied. "The sheriff told us someone deliberately drowned Buford. There were signs of a struggle around the hot tub, he said."

A silence fell over the startled group. Walt was the first to speak.

"What a shocker."

The others nodded, stunned and speechless for a few moments.

"The sheriff said he'd be making a statement soon," Sophie said. "Then he'll interview everyone who was on the premises last night, starting with those who were at the penthouse party."

Larry scowled. "The sheriff should concentrate on the people who were at the party and not waste his time bothering anyone else."

"I agree," Dennis said. "I hope we all don't have to hang around the lobby most of the day waiting to be questioned."

"We were set to tee off right after breakfast," Walt added. "But maybe we should forget about that now, anyway, out of respect . . ."

Larry gave a mirthless laugh. "*Respect?* For that louse?"

The other three ignored the remark. They must be used to Larry bad-mouthing Buford Doakes, Liz thought. Again, she wondered why Larry had such an intense dislike for Buford.

Just then the waitress brought the water bottles for Liz and Sophie. "Enjoy your hike," she said.

"Looks like you two are ready to go," Walt said. "I hope the sheriff doesn't keep you waiting long for your interviews."

"We've already been interviewed," Sophie said.

"Didn't you say he was going to start with the people who were at the party?" Jim asked.

"We were at the party," Liz replied.

The four of them stared in surprise. Walt broke into a grin. "So that's why you were in such a hurry to get away from us last night."

"How come you didn't tell us you'd been invited to the big bash?" Dennis added.

"We didn't get invited till we left you guys and were on our way to our room," Liz explained. She described how Buford's manager had approached them in the lobby.

"At first we didn't intend to go . . ." Sophie began.

Larry broke in. "But you couldn't pass up a chance to party with Mr. Dimples, could you?" He cast them a scrutinizing look. "You don't look as if you'd spent most of last night in a hot tub with him."

"We passed on that," Liz replied. "We left the party early."

"Smart cookies," Larry said, with a wry smile.

How did he know about Buford's bikini party? Liz wondered. On second thought, she realized Buford's penchant for hot tub frolicking was no secret.

"If it turns out we aren't allowed on the golf course and you aren't allowed out on the hiking trail, maybe we could get together after breakfast," Walt suggested. "Go for a swim or play cards or something."

"The sheriff told us we could do what we liked as long as we didn't leave the property," Sophie said.

"So we're going to hit the brookside trail in a few minutes," Liz added. "I'm sure the golf course isn't off limits. You can play if you want to." She glanced at Larry, remembering his caustic remark about showing respect for Buford.

"We'll discuss that while we eat," Walt said, as they turned to go.

"See you around," Sophie replied.

They watched the foursome go to their table. A few moments later they saw Gail come into the dining room, alone.

"I'll bet her three tennis pals are nursing huge hangovers," Sophie said.

"Especially the one Buford was hitting on," Liz replied.

"Yeah. Penny. I hope Gail didn't have too much trouble getting her out of Buford's clutches."

"Let's stop at her table on our way out," Liz said.

When they approached Gail's table, Liz noticed that Gail looked dazed and subdued. "I guess you heard the terrible story going around about Buford drowning in the hot tub and the police saying it wasn't an accident," she said. "It can't be true."

"Unfortunately, it's true," Liz replied. "We were in the lobby very early. The sheriff was there and he told us."

Gail looked surprised. "He did?"

"Yeah," Sophie added. "And we saw Buford being wheeled out in a body bag,"

Gail shuddered. "I was hoping it was just a rumor. Needless to say, we won't be playing tennis this morning." She gave a deep sigh. "Even if the others were up for it, I don't think any of us would have the heart to play. We weren't exactly big fans, but to have him die that way . . ." She shook her head and sighed again. "I can't believe someone deliberately drowned him when he was out of it with booze and pot. Who'd do something like that?"

"It had to be someone who was at the party," Sophie replied. "The sheriff's going to interview everyone who was there last night, and everyone who was on the inn property last night, too. He's all through with us. There weren't many other guests at the party. He'll get to you soon."

"Pedro, the bellman, told me the sheriff's been talking to Buford's manager and bodyguards and the rest of them," Gail said. "And he said the bodyguards and whoever else was sleeping in the penthouse were moved to rooms on a lower floor." She frowned. "A lot of good those bodyguards were."

"Most likely Buford went to bed and the bodyguards were sure he was in for the night, but he came out later for another drink and another dip in the tub," Liz said.

"I'll bet that's what happened," Gail said. "He was too high to go to sleep, and when he came out of his bedroom someone attacked him." She shook her head. "It's horrible."

To spare her further discomfort, Liz switched the subject. "How did it go with Penny after we left?"

"It was a hassle getting her away from him. Sue and Katie got out of the tub and got dressed, but he wouldn't let go of Penny. Sue and Katie went down to our rooms but I hung around. I finally got Penny out of the tub when a blond woman, I think she's part of his entourage, diverted Buford's attention."

Liz and Sophie exchanged glances. *That had to be Ms. Frizzy Hair.*

Buford might be partial to blond women, Liz thought. If Ms. Frizzy Hair was indeed his girlfriend, that made one. Gail's friend, Penny, made two. And Sophie would have made three if Buford had gotten her in his sights. She smiled, imagining him making moves on feisty Sophie.

"This has really ruined our weekend," Gail said. "Nothing to do all day but wait around for the sheriff to ask questions . . ."

"We're going hiking this morning," Liz said. "How about coming with us?"

"Oh, thanks, but I should stick around the inn in case I'm called for questioning," Gail replied. "Besides, I don't have the energy for a hike. I guess I'll just go to the pool and soak up some rays and wait for my friends." She paused. "Where are you going hiking?"

"There's a trail along the brook," Sophie said. "It goes up the hillside a couple of miles and doubles back to the lake shore."

"Well, enjoy yourselves," Gail said. "I'll see you later."

In the lobby, groups of stunned guests and unabashedly tearful groupies congregated, talking in hushed tones.

"Let's get out of here," Sophie said.

Heading for the exit, they ran into Pedro who greeted them with a smile and a pleasant "buenos días." But in the next instant, the smile faded. "You know what happen?" he asked.

"Yes," Liz replied. "We were in the lobby very early. The sheriff was there. He told us."

"The policia, he tell me very early, too," Pedro said.

"How come you were able to get here?" Sophie asked. "The sheriff told us the road into the property's been blocked."

"Me and some other help, we got rooms to sleep over kitchen," Pedro replied. "The policia, he tell us what happen when we start work." He sighed, shaking his head. "When I take food to penthouse last night, I see Buford having good time, and now. . . ." His face saddened.

Taking a late supper to the penthouse meant that Pedro had a very long day, Liz thought.

Evidently Sophie had the same thought. "That must have been well after midnight, Pedro," she said. "How come you were on duty so late?"

"I work late I get more pay," he replied. He eyed their backpacks and hiking boots and managed a wan smile. "You go for walk?"

"Right," Liz replied. "On the trail along the brook."

"You have good walk, señoritas," he said.

Chapter Six

They followed the rustic signs directing them to the brookside trail.

The sun had climbed higher into a clear, blue sky. The air still held the dewy fragrance of early morning. When they came to a footbridge, the murmur of the brook blended with songs of birds in the treetops.

On the bridge, they paused for a few moments, looking over the rail into the fast flowing stream, then gazing up the slope to the sun-dappled trail.

"What a beautiful spot," Liz said.

"Yeah, it's romantic," Sophie replied. "I wish the guys were here."

"Me too. You know what? We should call them and tell them about Buford. Did you bring your phone?"

Sophie patted her backpack. "Sure I did. I'll call Ralph and then you can call Ike."

A few minutes later she looked disappointed. "He's not picking up. Maybe he's in the shower." She handed the phone to Liz. "Here, you call Ike. I'll get through to Ralph after you've finished."

Ike picked up on the second ring. "Eichle here."

"Rooney here," she replied, smiling at the recollection of their former hostility. They'd come a long way since they'd called one another only by their last names. But not quite far enough, she thought, with an inward sigh.

"Liz! I didn't expect to hear from you till you got home. Everything okay?"

"Not exactly . . ." To head off any worrisome thoughts the words might have caused him, she hastened to tell him about Buford.

"Are you putting me on?" he asked.

"Absolutely not. He was found drowned in his hot tub in the wee hours this morning."

"And you say the local sheriff's calling it a homicide?"

"Right."

She heard something like a groan on the wire. "What was that for?" she asked.

"I hope you'll stay out of it," he replied.

"I have no intention of getting involved in the case," she said, slightly miffed.

"Well that would be a first."

"Just because I like getting involved in *your* cases doesn't mean I want to get into this one. Anyway, the sheriff seems to be on top of it."

"You've had direct contact with the sheriff?"

"Yes. Sophie and I talked with him early this morning. His name's MacDuff. When he found out Sophie's a cop, and Pop was a homicide detective, he couldn't have been nicer." She paused. "I just wanted to let you know about Buford before you heard it on the news. Sophie wants to call Ralph, so I'll say good-bye now."

"Good-bye Liz. Be careful," Ike said.

Liz knew that Ike would always be mindful of the predicaments she'd gotten herself into—some of them dangerous. She told herself there'd be no chance of that this weekend. Those dangerous situations had happened during her solitary sleuthing. She and Sophie were together this weekend, and she had no intention of snooping, anyway.

Sophie got through to Ralph. After informing him about Buford and talking for a few minutes, she said good-bye.

"Ralph told me to be careful," she said.

"Ike said the same thing to me. I hope they don't think I'm going to nose around up here and get you involved. Believe me, I have no such intention."

Sophie laughed. "Aren't you curious about who drowned poor Buford? Wouldn't you like to dig up some clues for Sheriff MacDuff?"

"Sure I'm curious, but there'll be none of that this weekend. I assured Ike I wouldn't get involved."

The trail led upward along the rushing stream. After awhile they came to a beautiful little waterfall, where they sat on a big rock to rest and enjoy the distant view of the lake.

"This must be one of the most unspoiled places in the state of Pennsylvania," Liz said.

"It hasn't changed much over the years," Sophie said. "I read in one of those pamphlets that very few trees were chopped down. The golf course was built mostly on meadowland, way back in the 1920s."

"Do you suppose early twentieth century sweethearts walked this trail and maybe sat on this very rock?" Liz asked.

"Yeah," Sophie said, "And I wish our twenty-*first* century sweethearts were here right now to enjoy the scenery with us. I know Ralph would love it here."

"Ike told me when he was a kid he used to spend summers near here on his grandparents' farm," Liz said. "He knows how beautiful this area is."

"Well, we better get going again," Sophie said. "I read in one of the pamphlets that it takes three to four hours to hike the whole trail. We want to get back to the inn in time for lunch."

They followed the trail from the top of the waterfall, upstream, till they came upon a section of the golf course. From a distant stand of trees, the brook rushed toward them, across a fairway. There, the trail turned. Across another footbridge, it began its descent to the lake.

They followed it, and stopped again, at the top of the waterfall, for a brief rest and a drink from their water bottles.

Liz realized it had been some time since she'd given any thought to Buford's death. It was as if the beauty of the brook and the woodland and the waterfall had transported her to a world apart from the ugliness of homicide.

"By the time the weekend's over, I might be a dedicated environmentalist," she said, as they made their way downward.

"Me too," Sophie replied.

"Gram remembers when many areas of Staten Island were wild and beautiful, like this," Liz said.

"Yeah—before it was torn up to build a bridge from Brooklyn and a highway right across the middle to New Jersey," Sophie agreed.

The sun was high by the time they reached the lakeshore. They paused to look out over the blue water where white sails skimmed and powerboats streaked.

"I wonder if the inn rents sailboats by the hour," Liz said. "I still remember how to handle sails from when I was dating the guy with the Star. Remember him?"

"Sure I do. That was the summer you spent every waking hour at the Great Kills Yacht Club. But if you're suggesting we rent a sailboat, I don't think MacDuff would allow it. Leaving the inn boat dock would be leaving the premises."

"Like Buford's killer would decide to make a getaway by sailboat," Liz said, with a laugh. She glanced through the trees toward the inn, about a ten minute walk from where they stood, and the swimming and boat docks below its broad verandahs. "Would we be leaving the premises if we went for a swim in the lake?" she asked.

"We'll ask MacDuff when we get back." Sophie replied.

"I'm not in any hurry to get back," Liz said. "By this time he must have put out the official word about Buford. Everyone will be looking glum, waiting to be questioned, talking about the murder and griping about the concert being cancelled and not being allowed to leave."

'And the groupies will be weeping and wailing," Sophie added. She checked her watch. "We have plenty of time before the dining room closes." She pointed to a large fallen log. "Let's hang out around here awhile."

Liz was about to seat herself on the log when something caught her eye. A few feet away on the slope of the hill, almost hidden in the dense foliage, she saw what appeared to be a crude wooden door.

"Up there in the woods, Sophie—could that be one of the old icehouses we read about?" she asked.

Sophie looked. "It might be. Let's go and see."

They made their way through the foliage, expecting to find a small structure. Instead, they found a cave. The door they'd glimpsed had been built across the opening. A rusty hasp, stuck with a stout piece of wood, secured its weathered boards to the sagging frame.

"I'll bet they used this cave as an icehouse," Sophie said.

"I'll bet they did, too. I wonder how far back into the hill it goes."

"Let's check it out." Sophie started sliding the stick from the hasp. It came out without too much effort. She placed it on the ground near the door.

"Oh, rats. there's no doorknob," she said. "How can we get the door open?"

Liz scrutinized the door. Besides having no knob, it had no visible hinges. "This door opens inward," she said. "All we have to do is push."

They put their shoulders against the weathered boards and pushed. The door creaked open. Light flooded in, revealing a large empty space. They could plainly see the remains of burlap bags and vestiges of straw.

"This was an icehouse, all right," Liz said. She propped a rock against the door to keep it open while they went in and looked around.

The cave had a dirt floor. Overhead it was solid rock. The side walls looked like a mixture of rock and earth. They walked to the back of the cave, a distance of about ten feet, Liz judged, and saw that the back wall appeared to be solid rock.

Sophie rubbed her hands over her arms. "Wow, what a difference in temperature. When they got all those blocks of ice in here it must have been like a freezer."

"It's hard to imagine life without modern refrigeration," Liz said. "But actually, it wasn't that long ago. Gram told me when she was a very little girl their house had sort of a shed off the kitchen where they had a wooden cabinet for perishable food, with a separate compartment lined with tin for the ice. A man used to drive around and look for a sign in people's front windows saying 'ice.' He'd carry the ice in with big tongs. Gram said there were holes in the bottom of the ice compartment and the floor of the shed, so when the ice melted it could drain out."

"I wish I had a grandmother alive to tell me things like that," Sophie said. She ran her hand over the back wall of the cave. "This rock is actually cold," she said. "Come here and feel it."

Just as Liz stepped over to examine the rock wall, they heard a loud bang. The cave went dark, and then came a scraping sound.

Sophie gasped. "The door's swung shut. Let's get it open, quick."

How could the door have swung shut when it had a rock propped against it? Liz wondered, as they groped their way to the front of the cave.

Guided by chinks of light around the frame, they found the door. Liz fumbled around, hoping the inside knob was still intact. In a few moments her hands came upon it.

"Good," she said, giving it a pull. The door didn't budge.

"It must be stuck," Sophie said. Liz noticed a slight tremor in her voice.

"I don't see how it could be stuck. There's enough space between the door and the frame for light to come in," Liz said.

She and Sophie both pulled the knob again. When the door still didn't move, Liz felt a pang of apprehension. "It feels as if it's locked," she said. "Do you suppose someone from the inn was walking by and noticed the door was wide open, so he closed it and put the stick back in the hasp?"

Through the darkness, she heard Sophie take a deep breath. "The door's almost hidden up here in the trees and brush," she replied. "You wouldn't have seen it if we hadn't stopped right below it and you happened to look up into the woods. Forget about someone walking by and noticing the door open. I think someone's been following us and deliberately locked us in here."

Chapter Seven

Sophie was right, Liz thought. The scraping sound she'd heard was the stick being put back in the hasp. She felt a stab of apprehension, but an instant later she remembered Sophie's cell phone. They could call for help.

Sophie's voice came through the darkness. "Oh, Liz, it's so dark in here . . ." Suddenly, she sounded like a scared child.

Liz knew why. Sophie had told her about an early childhood incident when she'd hidden in a closet during a game of hide and seek. The closet door had no inside knob. By the time she was found, the damage had been done. A fear of the dark and of closed spaces had plagued her ever since.

The phobias had lessened as she matured. "Mostly because I learned to avoid situations that would bring them on," Sophie had told her.

Minutes ago the cave had been flooded with light from the wide open door. There'd been no reason for Sophie to think they would suddenly be plunged into darkness and she'd become a frightened four-year-old again.

With the few slivers of light from around the door piercing the blackness, Liz reached for Sophie's backpack. "Hang in there," she said. "We have your phone. I can't remember the inn number, but I'll call 911. They'll contact the inn and someone will come and get us out of here. Meanwhile, keep looking at the chinks of light around the door."

She grabbed the phone out of Sophie's backpack. To her dismay, it didn't work. *I should have known*, she thought. *We're underground, surrounded by rock.* She felt almost paralyzed by apprehension. *What are we going to do?*

Sophie's trembling voice came into the silence. "The phone's dead, isn't it? It won't work in here."

Admitting this would add to Sophie's distress, but she had to do it. "Yes," she said. Then, trying to keep Sophie from knowing she too was scared, she added, "But I'm sure there'll be other hikers coming along the trail. We'll listen for them and when we hear them we'll yell." *If they could hear footsteps or voices from up here.*

Sophie took a deep breath and leaned against the door where the light shone through. It was as if those minute rays were barely keeping her from going to pieces.

A sudden idea sent Liz delving into Sophie's backpack where she'd noticed Sophie putting her jack knife. Attached to the knife was a tiny flashlight. Small as the light would be, it might be a comfort.

The instant the miniscule light came on, Sophie turned to it like a storm-harried ship toward a beacon. Liz could hear relief in her long sigh.

Seconds later, Sophie managed a feeble laugh. "Can you believe this? A tough NYPD cop afraid of being locked up in the dark? I gotta pull myself together."

Sophie, beset with her phobias, was trying to pull herself together, and so should she, Liz decided. She put knife and flashlight on the ground and got Sophie's water bottle out of her backpack. Sophie took a drink and handed it back.

"Thanks."

"Feeling better?"

"Yeah." Sophie sat down on the ground near the flashlight and as close to the door as she could get. "I'm okay. We might as well take off our backpacks. Looks like we might be here for awhile. Let's try and figure things out and decide what we should do."

A wave of relief washed over Liz. Sophie seemed to be okay. Without her strength and support, for a few dreadful minutes she'd come close to panic herself. She was still scared, but now they were a team, again—Pulaski and Rooney, who'd so often talked about becoming private investigators.

"This is a job for a couple of savvy Private Eyes," she said. "First, who locked us in here and why?"

"I have a hunch it has something to do with Buford's murder," Sophie replied. "Someone at the inn besides the sheriff must have found out I'm a New York cop, and decided you're a cop, too. Most likely whoever found this out thinks we're both detectives and wanted us out of the way while the interviews are going on."

"You figure the killer would rather have Sheriff MacDuff investigating the case without the help of two sharp NYPD detectives?" Liz asked.

"Exactly. I think whoever drowned Buford is counting on MacDuff being a country bumpkin lawman who'd bungle the case if he handled it all by himself."

"But what led the killer to believe we're a couple of sleuths? I'm sure the sheriff didn't shoot off his mouth that you're a NYPD cop."

"The night clerk could have picked it up when we were talking with the sheriff. He could have spread the word, and by the time the story got to the killer, we were both detectives."

"Or maybe it was Pedro," Liz said. "Remember, in the parking lot we were talking about you flashing your badge and gun?"

"Oh, that's right. We were opening the trunk and didn't see him till he spoke to us. He must have overheard us."

"Either he or the night clerk could have started spreading the story that two New York cops were staying at the inn. So, by the time we were ready for our hike, a lot of people might have gotten the word that we're both NYPD homicide detectives, on the case with the sheriff," Liz said. "Now the question is, who besides the Lexus guys and Gail knew exactly where we were going to hike?"

"On the way out we told Pedro we were taking the brookside trail."

Liz sensed Sophie staring at her through the darkness. "Are you thinking what I'm thinking?" Sophie asked.

"Yes, if you're thinking Pedro told us he was in the penthouse late last night, delivering food."

"Yeah. Being in the penthouse late last night doesn't exactly put him at the scene of the crime, but it's something to consider."

"Maybe we shouldn't be so quick to eliminate him as a suspect. He could have hidden somewhere up there till everyone left and waited for a chance to get Buford alone."

"That would be difficult, with Buford's bodyguards there. Besides, why would Pedro want to kill Buford? As far as we know, he'd never laid eyes on him till this weekend."

It seemed as if discussing the case had diverted Sophie's mind away from her phobias, Liz thought. It had lessened her own tension, too, although there were moments when the reality of their situation sent daggers of fear into her heart.

"As far as we know there's no connection between Buford and Pedro," she said. "But Pedro seemed to know an awful lot about the people Buford brought with him."

"Yeah, he did. But most likely he's just a busybody who has to know everything that goes on at the inn." Sophie turned the flashlight on her wristwatch. "If we hadn't gotten ourselves in this mess, we'd be back at the inn by now having lunch. I wonder if anyone has noticed we're missing."

"I'll bet the Lexus guys have. Maybe they'll tell the sheriff and he'll organize a search party," Liz said. With this thought, her imagination took off. "But what if the sheriff thinks we're missing because we had something to do with the murder? What if he thinks you showed him a fake ID and you're not a cop at all? What if he thinks we used our hike as a pretext to flee? He could believe we linked up with a cohort on the golf course who got us away in a golf cart to a car waiting on some remote country road . . ."

Sophie broke in. "And the sheriff will launch a statewide manhunt. They'll search everywhere but never think of looking for us on inn property. We'll be trapped in here forever and die of starvation or hypothermia, or both, and nobody will ever know what happened to us." Her laugh came through the darkness, telling Liz she was kidding.

"Your imagination's almost as wild as mine," Liz said. Sophie couldn't have joked and laughed about their situation if she were still in the full grip of her phobias. Or was laughing in the dark like whistling in the dark?

"With all the excitement about Buford's murder, who's going to notice we didn't show up for lunch?" Sophie asked. "We shouldn't count on anyone looking for us. We should concentrate on getting out of here. There's gotta be a way. If we think hard enough we'll come up with something."

Knowing Sophie always kept her gun with her gave Liz an idea. "With chinks of light coming in around the door, we can figure where the hasp is. Could you fire some shots at that area and break through the door so we could reach the hasp?"

"The old John Wayne maneuver?" Sophie asked. "If I had a shotgun, I'd blast that door in a minute, but my service gun wouldn't do the job." She paused. "I suppose I could fire a few shots on the faint chance of someone passing by hearing them, but I'd rather save the ammunition."

Liz was about to ask Sophie why she wanted to save ammunition, when an idea struck her. "It's so frustrating, seeing that light coming in around the door, especially near the place where the hasp is," she said. "Is there any way we could pry at the wood and make an opening big enough to stick a hand through and get at the hasp?"

"Good thinking," Sophie replied. "My jack knife's small, but it's sharp. It'll take time, but eventually it could slice away enough wood for us to get at the hasp." She detached the flashlight from the knife. "Let's take turns; I'll go first. You hold the light so I can see what I'm doing."

Sophie got to work. "If the killer believes he put us out of the way for good, he's got another thing coming," she said.

"If he only wants us out of the way while the sheriff is do-ing the interviews, maybe he intends to sneak back here and let us out before we starve to death," Liz said.

"Ha!" Sophie replied, whittling at the weathered wood

plank closest to where the hasp would be. "Anyone vicious enough to drown a guy under the influence of drugs and alcohol is vicious enough to leave two women to die in a cave."

Liz pondered this. When the killer followed them on their hike, he or she didn't know they were going into the cave. Locking them in seemed like an impulsive act, carried out without any thought of consequences. Perhaps the drowning, too, had been done without forethought. And why had they been followed, anyway? Did the killer hope to overhear talk about the murder and learn who the suspects were?

"This wood is hard as a rock," Sophie said. "I'm not making much headway. This is going to take awhile but it's going to get us out of here before night."

She was determined to get out of the cave while light still shone around the door. At least seven more hours, Liz judged. By then they might have an opening big enough for a hand to fit through and get the stick out of the hasp.

It was slow going. When Liz shone the flashlight on her watch, they'd been working for nearly two hours and the space hadn't even widened enough for their fingertips. At this rate they'd never make it. She shook her head. *Don't think like that.* For Sophie's sake, they had to get out of there by dusk.

A sudden, chilling thought popped into her mind. *Snakes.* When the sun went down, would they come slithering through the space between the ground and the bottom of the door? Now she knew why Sophie wanted to save the ammunition!

Sophie's voice interrupted the frightening thought. "I think the opening's getting a little bigger, but this wood's really hard."

Were all the planks in the door that same hard wood? Liz wondered. She looked away from the small opening and glanced over the rest of the door. In the area around it, there was scarcely enough light coming through to be called slivers, but she was able to make out three wide-strap hinges.

Maybe the wood was softer in the planks the hinges were on. Maybe, over the years, the hinges had loosened. Her mind leaped ahead. She pictured them getting the two lower hinges off and then manipulating the door, creating a space big enough for them to squeeze out. The top hinge, left intact, would keep the door from falling on them.

The idea excited her. She ran it by Sophie, who immediately stopped what she was doing. "It's worth a try," she said.

They played the flashlight over the planks where the lower hinges were. Sophie hacked at the area with her knife. "Good," she said. "This wood's softer."

The hinges were slightly rusted, and firmly attached. But with this softer wood, they might be able to get the screws out, Liz thought—that is if Sophie's knife could do the job.

"There's a screwdriver with my knife," Sophie said. "Too bad it's not very big, but it will have to do. We'll see if the screws come out easily. If it turns out to be a hassle, we'll go back to plan one."

Liz held the flashlight. Sophie tried to loosen the screws.

"They're rusted in there pretty tight," she said. "If we only had some solvent or something, I think they'd come out with a little work."

"I might have a small bottle of club soda in my backpack, left over from the last time I used it," Liz said.

Sophie's voice brightened. "I've heard that works."

"Gram swears by it," Liz said. She groped around in her backpack and found the bottle. "I'll sprinkle it around the screws and leave it on for a while to give it a chance to dissolve the rust."

"While we're waiting, we'll keep hacking away at the wood near the hasp. That'll double our chances of getting out of here," Sophie said.

Their chances of getting through to the hasp before dusk were slim, Liz thought. The opening was scarcely half an inch wide. She thought about Ike. He'd never quit teasing her about this—that is, if she were ever able to tell him. She shoved this worst-case scenario out of her mind and continued to take turns working on the wood. At least the slightly widened crack was bringing in a bit more light.

She'd felt hungry for awhile before Sophie mentioned she was, too. "Lucky we brought along granola bars," Sophie said.

"I wish we had more than two," Liz replied. "Let's share one now and save the other one in case we need it, later." She thrust away the thought that 'later' might mean that night or even tomorrow.

They ate one granola bar and drank some water. Liz noticed the bottles were getting close to empty. A dagger of fear stabbed at her heart. She tried to ignore it.

"It's been more than an hour since we doused the screws," she said. "Shall we see if they've loosened?"

In the bottom hinge, two out of the three screws were loose. Sophie managed to remove one. They wet the two remaining screws liberally with club soda, then checked the other hinge. Two screws came right out. The third one wouldn't budge. They poured club soda on the stubborn one.

"We'll wait awhile," Sophie said. "When we get back to them they should all be easy to get out."

They probably would, Liz thought, but after the hinges came off they'd have to tug at the door to get a space big enough for them to wriggle through. It would be a struggle and they'd both wind up with splinters in their hands. But splinters were preferable to snakebites, she decided, with a shudder.

Despite their encouragement concerning the hinges, Sophie insisted on going back to hacking at the hard wood. After they'd each taken a couple of turns, Liz began to feel weary. "I think we could both use some rest," she said. "Let's knock off for awhile."

"Okay, I admit I'm beat, but let's not fall asleep," Sophie replied.

Sophie didn't want to oversleep and wake up and see no daylight coming through the opening, Liz thought. And *she* didn't want to wake up to the hissing of snakes—maybe even a rattle.

"If we keep talking we won't fall asleep," she said.

They stretched out on the ground close to the door, using their backpacks as head pillows. Sophie put the flashlight on the ground between them, but turned it off so the batteries wouldn't die.

"What do you suppose is happening back at the inn?" she asked.

"The sheriff has announced Buford's death as a homicide," Liz replied. "And by now the news is probably all over the radio and TV."

"I guess the inn is swarming with reporters," Sophie said. A moment later she added, "Oh, I forgot the sheriff told us state troopers have blocked the road and nobody can get in or out till he's finished his interviewing."

"Speaking of the sheriff—don't you think by this time someone might have mentioned we're missing?" Liz asked. "He could have sent someone out to look for us."

"If he did, we would have been rescued by now," Sophie said. "Maybe your idea of him thinking we took it on the lam isn't so crazy after all." She sounded drowsy, Liz thought.

"Quit your kidding, Sophie. If a search party was out looking for us they could have walked right past this patch of woods without noticing the door to the cave. You remember we wouldn't have seen it if we hadn't stopped right there for a few minutes."

Sophie didn't reply. Her measured breathing told Liz she was asleep.

She was exhausted, both from her battle with her phobias and from their physical work, Liz thought. She decided to let Sophie sleep as long as she needed to, but she'd stay awake to make sure they got back to the hinges in an hour or so. She'd just close her eyes and relax.

She wasn't certain how much time had passed before her eyes flew open and she realized she, too, had fallen asleep. Sophie showed no signs of awakening.

Liz didn't need to turn on the flashlight and check her

watch to know they'd slept away the afternoon. The light coming through the opening on the door was the deep golden color of early evening, just before sunset.

She grabbed the flashlight and sprang to her feet. *The rust around the remaining screws should be dissolved by now*, she thought, playing the light over them. They'd left Sophie's knife on the ground nearby. She picked it up and started to work on one of the screws in the bottom hinge. After ten minutes or so, it came out.

Her squeal of excitement awoke Sophie. "Have you been working while I've been asleep?" she asked.

"I confess I fell asleep, too," Liz said. "I haven't been working very long."

"Well, thanks for not waking me up. I feel great, except I'm starved."

"Me too," Liz replied. "But we'd better not finish the last granola bar yet. Let's get to work on the last screw in the bottom hinge."

"Have you noticed it's always the last one you have trouble with?" Sophie asked, after they'd both worked on it for awhile. She handed the screwdriver to Liz. "Here, you try again."

A few passes and the screw came out. They hugged each other in jubilation.

Liz hoped that Sophie was too happy to notice the light coming through the cracks was not as bright as before. *The sun must be close to setting*, she thought. "Now for the rest of those screws," she said, forcing a cheerful note into her voice.

They took turns working on the screws in the middle hinge. By the time all of them came out, and they'd pried at the hinges with the knife and swung them out of the way, the light around the door had dimmed even more.

If Sophie noticed, she said nothing about it. "Are we ready for the big heave ho?" she asked.

With the flashlight's feeble ray and diminishing light from around the door, they located its lower side. Liz's heart sank. She should have realized that heaving the door inward wasn't going to be easy. There wasn't enough space between the door and jamb.

"How are we going to pull at the door?" she asked. "We have nothing to grab onto."

"Maybe we can work from the bottom," Sophie said. She shone the flashlight on the small space between the door and ground. "If we only had something to dig with . . ."

"Even if we did, this dirt is hard as rock," Liz said. "It might *be* mostly rock."

Sophie played the light over the slivers of space around the door. "What I wouldn't do for a crowbar," she muttered. A moment later she gave a grunt. "My gun's gotta be good for something besides shooting," she said. "If I could just get the barrel wedged between the door and the jamb, I could pry it open enough for us to get our hands in there and grab hold."

Liz was sure there wasn't nearly enough space to wedge the gun. When she heard Sophie sigh, she knew Sophie realized this, too.

Liz was struck with an idea. "If we sliced some of the wood away from the door like we were doing in the other area, we could open up a space for the gun barrel."

"Now why didn't I think of that?" Sophie asked.

They took turns with the knife working on the lower part of the door. The softer wood whittled off easily.

"This is almost as good as a crowbar," Sophie said, wedging the barrel of her gun into the opening. Within a few moments she pried a space big enough for their hands. They both took hold of the edge. In unison, they pulled with all their strength. The door creaked but it didn't budge.

"All we're going to get out of this is a fistful of splinters," Liz said. "Pulling isn't going to work. Pushing would put more pressure on the door. Maybe if we could get our hands around to the outside . . ."

Sophie worked her gun barrel into the widened crack, again. After a few minutes she'd pried an opening that looked large enough for their hands and wrists to reach the outside of the door. This would have lightened the cave considerably if it hadn't been late in the day, Liz thought.

"Let's get going on the big push," Sophie said. "But before we try it out we should take our socks off and put them over our hands. We don't want our palms bristling with century-old splinters."

With sockless feet in their boots, and makeshift mittens on their hands, they worked their hands and wrists into the opening, flattened their palms against the other side of the door and tried to push. But the angle was awkward for applying pressure.

Sophie got busy with her gun barrel again. "If I keep prying, maybe I can make an opening large enough for us to get out," she said.

Sure, if she worked on it for another hour or two, Liz thought. By that time it could be pitch dark outside and the cave floor crawling with snakes. The thought gave her the creeps. "Never mind waiting for an opening big enough for us to crawl through," she said. "The minute you see a space each of us can get one forearm into, let's go for another push."

"Good idea," Sophie said. "The extra pressure of arms and elbows might get this damn door moving—if we can figure a good way to position ourselves. Meanwhile, I'll pry the space. Lucky neither of us has beefy arms."

With renewed vigor, she got to work again. Liz heard the weathered wood of frame and door gradually yield to the prying gun barrel. Much sooner than either of them expected, more light came through an opening that looked big enough.

Sophie tried it out and was able to get a hand and an arm up to her elbow around to the other side of the door in a kind of awkward embrace. "I never thought I'd be hugging a door," she said, pushing it. It creaked but it didn't move.

"We need to hug it together," Liz said.

After much maneuvering and getting in each other's way, they found it impossible for each to fit an arm into the opening at the same time.

"This is so frustrating," Sophie said. Through the semi-darkness, Liz saw her give the door a swift kick.

The sound of Sophie's boot against the door gave Liz an idea. "Let's forget about moving the door inward," she said. "Let's try getting it to go sort of sideways. If I can get my feet between the door and the jamb, I could push against the lower side of the door, sideways, while you hug the upper part and . . ."

"I'll try anything to get out of here," Sophie said.

Liz flopped to the ground next to the lower part of the jamb. Lying on her side, she worked her feet, one above the other, into the opening, firming them against the side of the door.

Sophie played the flashlight over her. "Okay, while you're down there pushing sideways, I can be doing a forward and sideways hug maneuver from up here."

"Right," Liz said. She dug her left elbow into the ground and further braced herself with her right hand and arm.

She heard Sophie positioning herself above, then her voice. "Ready?"

"Yes, all set."

"On the count of three—one, two, go!"

The door shuddered. Liz could feel a slight motion. "It's working!" she exclaimed.

They tried again. Liz felt the door giving way to the pressure of her feet and legs. "It moved! Did you feel it?" she asked. "And there's more light!"

"Yeah," Sophie replied. "I can see you. Really, Liz, you should do something about your hair."

Liz could hear relief in the quip. Sophie had been suppressing her panic all this time, but didn't want her to know. "Like you're Miss America?" she retorted.

They tried once more, giving it all they had. This time the door gave a lurch and slid sideways on an inward angle. A wide ray of late-day light flooded into the cave.

Sophie took one look at the size of the opening and gave a yelp of delight. She grabbed her gun, went flat on her belly and wriggled through.

Liz controlled her impulse to get out of there on Sophie's

heels. Instead, she scooped up knife and flashlight and put them in Sophie's backpack with the phone. Then she shoved both backpacks out through the opening and crawled through.

Nothing had ever looked so beautiful as that first glimpse of trees and sky in the lingering daylight, nor felt so good as that first sweet breath of outdoor air.

Chapter Eight

Outside, in the gathering dusk, they hugged each other, danced around and laughed. They took off their boots, and slid their feet into their socks. They put on their boots and strapped on their backpacks.

Liz looked down the trail toward the inn. "A quick shower and change and we'll make it to the dining room before it closes," she said.

"And not a minute too soon," Sophie replied. "My stomach's growling."

"Oh, was that you?" Liz asked, as they started along the path. "I thought we were in trouble again with a wild animal about to attack us."

Sophie laughed. "Very funny. But after what we've been through, taking on a wild animal would be easy." She patted her pocket where she'd put her gun.

"I hope there won't be a crowd in the lobby," Liz said. "They'll wonder what we've been doing to get ourselves so filthy."

"This is one time when telling the truth wouldn't be advisable," Sophie replied. "Nobody would believe a word of it."

Liz nodded. "Let's hope most of the guests will be in the dining room and we can slip onto the elevator unnoticed." She gave a sigh. "A hot shower is going to feel like heaven."

They quickened their pace. A few minutes later they

reached the parking area. While hurrying toward the entrance, they saw the sheriff's vehicle.

"Looks like MacDuff spent all day interviewing and he's probably still at it," Liz said. "I guess after we've cleaned up we should let him know we've come back—just in case he heard we've been gone since early morning. And of course we have to tell him what happened to us."

"I'm sure he'll agree this has something to do with Buford's murder," Sophie said. "Maybe he'll want to check the hasp and the stick for prints."

They went inside and headed straight for the elevators hoping none of the few people in the lobby would notice two grimy and bedraggled figures.

"So far so good," Liz said, as they waited for an elevator. "I don't want to talk to anyone till I'm cleaned up."

"Don't look around," Sophie warned. "The Lexus guys might be in the lobby. If they see us, they'll be over here in a split second."

The elevator came and they got on. As the doors were closing, Liz thought she glimpsed two men running across the lobby toward the elevators. "I think two of the Lexus guys saw us," she told Sophie, as the doors shut. "I couldn't tell which ones, but they were heading in this direction. I suppose I should have been courteous and held the doors open for them."

"I'm glad you didn't," Sophie replied. "They're probably wondering where we've been all day and we don't need to be bombarded with questions, at least not till we're showered and changed."

Liz gave a wry smile. "I feel as if I haven't had a bath in six months."

"Me too," Sophie replied. "If Ralph saw me looking like this, he'd call off the wedding."

"And Ike would call off any intentions he might have of popping the question," Liz added, with a laugh.

They'd been in their room only a few minutes, and had just taken their boots off, when a knock came at the door.

"The Lexus guys, I'll bet," Liz said.

Sophie grimaced. "Don't answer. Pretend we're not here."

After a moment, the knock sounded again, and with it, a voice that sent Liz's heart into a spin. "Police! Open up!"

She ran to the door, pulled it open and rushed into Ike's waiting arms.

It took a few seconds for her to realize that Ralph was there, too, and Sophie was also being hugged and kissed.

She hadn't planned to parody the question Ike had so often asked her during their hostile mode. It just slipped out.

"What are you doing here, Eichle?"

Sophie burst into peals of laughter. "Good one, Liz!"

But Ike and Ralph weren't laughing. By this time they'd taken in Liz and Sophie's sorry state.

"You have some explaining to do," Ralph said.

"Yeah, we need answers," Ike added. "Where have you been since eight o'clock this morning that got you looking like something the cat dragged in?"

Liz's first impulse was to relate their harrowing experience in detail. She wanted more than anything, at that moment, to feel Ike's arms around her again, to feel safe and loved, and be told he was proud of her courage and resourcefulness. But on second thought, she knew by the time their ordeal was described, the inevitable questions answered, and they'd had their showers and dressed, the dining room would be closed. And she felt almost weak with hunger.

She held back the words she longed to say. "It's too much to tell you now—right, Sophie?" she asked. She was counting on Sophie's growling stomach to back her up.

Sophie didn't let her down. "Right. We need to get cleaned up and down to the dining room. We're starved."

Ike cast them each a stern look. "Yeah, you need to get cleaned up, all right, and I know you're hungry," he said. "You've been hiking since early morning and you didn't have any lunch."

"We thought maybe you'd taken along a picnic, but we were told you hadn't ordered any food to go," Ralph added. "You owe us an explanation."

"You guys are the ones who sprung this surprise by showing up here. How about *you* doing some explaining?" Liz asked.

"But make it short," Sophie said, glancing at her watch.

Ike plucked a piece of wood shaving out of Liz's hair. "All right. After Liz called me and told me about Buford's murder, I thought of something I wanted to ask her. I figured you'd get back from your hike in time for lunch, so I called the inn around noon, but you weren't back yet. I knew Sophie would have her cell phone, so I called Ralph and got her number, but I couldn't get through."

"When Ike called me back and said he couldn't get anything on Sophie's phone, I tried it myself," Ralph said. "When I couldn't get through, either, I sensed something was wrong. Sophie always keeps her phone turned on."

Liz could see the puzzlement in Ike's eyes when he looked at her. "I called the inn again and asked the desk clerk to be sure and have you phone me the minute you returned. He promised he would. When I didn't get a call by two-thirty, I phoned the inn again and was told your room didn't answer. I asked the clerk to find out if you'd been in the dining room for lunch, and I waited while he checked. When it turned out you hadn't been in the dining room since breakfast, I thought it was strange you'd be out hiking for six hours without any lunch."

"Ike called me and told me," Ralph said. "We were both worried as hell, and we decided to drive up here. I put in for emergency time."

"And I took some time I had coming," Ike added. "We got here about five and contacted Sheriff MacDuff. He'd been busy interviewing and didn't know you'd been gone since early morning."

"We figured with the homicide he had enough on his mind without this, so we didn't make a big deal of it," Ralph said. "We decided to get out there and look for you. By that time the word had gotten out that you were overdue from your hike, and a young man offered to help us look for you. He said he'd check the lower trail while Ike and I hit the upper parts."

The man searching the lower trail must have passed right by the icehouse, calling their names while they were asleep, Liz decided.

"We hadn't been back long when we spotted you waiting for the elevator," Ike said. "You want to get cleaned up, so we'll take off now. We'll all get filled in on everything else, later."

"We'll meet you in the lobby in an hour and we'll grab some dinner before the dining room closes," Ralph added.

"Wait a second," Sophie said. "How did you guys get onto the inn property? The sheriff told us the road is blocked."

"Now it's our turn to say it would take too long," Ralph replied.

"We'll explain over dinner," Ike said. He gave Liz a quick kiss and headed for the door, where he waited a minute for Ralph and Sophie to come out of an embrace. "We'll see you downstairs," he said as he and Ralph left.

Sophie started to peel off her clothes. "They drove all the way up here because they were worried about us," she said. "I like it!"

"I like it, too," Liz replied. That was an understatement, she thought. From the moment she'd heard Ike's voice at the door, she'd been in a daze of delight. But she wasn't looking forward to telling Ike what happened. This would be one more predicament for him to remind her of. And, though she'd assured him she wasn't going to get involved in this case, the situation had changed. After their ordeal, how could she not be involved?

A familiar feeling of excitement and challenge came over her. She felt the stirring of her passion for following sensational murder cases and digging up clues. She knew she wanted to be involved in this one.

A further thought came to her. In her recent sleuthing, she'd had Ike's input. Would there be any chance of that, now? How would a country sheriff react to a big city detective's offer of help? Though he'd admitted he needed assistance, he might resent it. And maybe Ike wasn't keen on getting involved in it, anyway. Much as she wanted to jump right into this case, she couldn't do it without Ike.

Sophie's voice came into her musing. "How do you suppose Ralph and Ike got past the road block?"

Liz drove her last thoughts into a corner of her mind and told herself she'd get back to them very soon. She let the matter of Ike and Ralph running the blockade take over. "After they showed their police ID's, they probably talked the state troopers into letting them through," she replied.

Sophie shook her head. "I don't think the troopers would go for a couple of out of state, big city cops throwing their weight around against the local sheriff's orders."

"Well, Ike said he'd explain during dinner," Liz replied. "Right now I'm more hungry than curious. We better get cracking so we can get down to the dining room in time. You want to hit the shower first?"

"Okay. I'll make it as quick as I can, but I want to wash my hair."

"Me too."

"I'll be in and out in fifteen," Sophie said, on her way into the bathroom.

Less than an hour later, Liz in a turquoise blue cotton skirt and jacket, and Sophie in a pink linen dress, stepped off the elevator into the lobby where Ike and Ralph were waiting.

Ralph gave Sophie a hug. "Darling, you look beautiful— you, too, Liz."

"Right," Ike said. Liz knew he wasn't big on compliments, but couldn't he have managed one of his own, just this once? She was somewhat soothed when he kissed her. Actions speaking louder than words?

On the way into the dining room, Ike told Liz they'd talked to the sheriff. "He was pleased you got back okay. He was about to go home and he said he wouldn't be back till tomorrow morning."

"Did he finish his interviewing?" Sophie asked.

"I didn't ask," Ike replied.

Liz's heart sank. That meant he wasn't interested in the case.

"Looks like almost everybody ate early," Sophie said, as they entered the almost empty dining room. There was no sign of Gail or the Lexus quartette or any of Buford's entourage.

After they were seated, Ike looked up from perusing the menu. "How about shrimp cocktails to start, and then nice, thick steaks all around, with mushrooms and baked potatoes with sour cream, and big salads?"

Ralph nodded. "Suits me. And how about a bottle of Merlot?"

"I'll go for the whole works," Sophie said.

Liz gave Ike a grateful smile. He'd sensed she and Sophie were too hungry to want to scan the menu and decide. "Sounds wonderful," she said.

After they ordered, Sophie gave a sigh. "One more hour in that dark cave and I'd have had hallucinations about a big, juicy steak." The words were barely spoken before she shot a look at Liz. "Oh, well, we were going to tell them about it pretty soon, anyway," she said.

Ike and Ralph stared at her.

Ike leveled a stern gaze at Liz. "Is that where you were all day—exploring a cave?"

"Actually it was an old icehouse," Liz replied.

Sophie cut in. "And we weren't exactly exploring. We saw this cave that was used as an icehouse years ago, and we went inside to look around and someone locked us in."

"Locked you in!" Ralph exclaimed.

Ike frowned. "Are you sure you didn't accidentally lock yourselves in there?"

Liz described the hasp-and-stick locking device. "And Sophie took the stick out of the hasp and put it on the ground near the door," she said. "The door opened inward. I propped it with a rock. It couldn't have swung shut. Someone sneaked in, closed the door and put the stick back in the hasp."

Ralph cast Sophie a look, as if he didn't know whether

to empathize with her or be angry. "Sophie, you should have known better than to go into a dark cave," he growled. Clearly, he knew about Sophie's nyctophobia and claustrophobia.

"It wasn't dark when we went in. The door was very wide, so there was plenty of light inside," Sophie said. "We were in the back of the cave talking about old-fashioned refrigeration, when all of a sudden the door slammed shut . . ." Her voice faltered. Liz knew she was recalling her panic.

Sophie pulled herself together quickly. "But it wasn't bad," she continued. "There were chinks of light in places around the door and I had my little flashlight."

Ike looked grim. "The sheriff needs to be told about this," he said. "If I didn't know he'd been here since before dawn and needs a break, I'd phone him at his home tonight."

"Yeah, better wait till tomorrow," Ralph said. He paused. "Ike, they got us so wrought up about being locked in the cave, we never asked how they made it out."

Ike nodded. "That's right, we didn't." He looked at Liz and Sophie. "Okay, let's hear how you managed to get out of a locked cave in the middle of the woods."

Liz and Sophie took turns describing their efforts to escape.

"Looks like we got ourselves a couple of feisty chicks," Ralph said with a grin.

Ike nodded. "We have to keep an eye on them, though. It won't be long before whoever locked them in there is going to know they escaped. We don't want any more attempts to get them out of the way."

"Who'd want them out of the way, and why?" Ralph asked.

After Sophie and Liz expressed their thoughts about this, Ike and Ralph agreed whoever locked them up was most likely Buford's killer and he'd done this to keep them from helping the sheriff interview the suspects.

"This doesn't sound like the work of a clever criminal," Ike said. "He might have planned to sneak back to the cave, eventually, and unlock the door, but didn't he realize when you got out you'd go straight to the sheriff, and he'd find out who went out on the trail right after you did? Whoever did this didn't think things through."

"I don't believe he was ever going to unlock the cave door," Sophie said. "He counted on our bodies never being found and the murder developing into a cold case."

The waitress brought their dinners. After she left, Liz said she agreed with Ike. The perpetrator wasn't a clever criminal and might have planned to let them out, eventually. "Besides, how could the case go cold?" she asked. "It isn't as if the sheriff would have to launch an APB. The killer is right here at the inn, most likely someone who was at the party." And from all indications, hadn't thought things through with any degree of smarts.

Pop used to say if a detective didn't have some idea where a case was headed during the first twenty-four hours post homicide, it could be a long investigation. Had Sheriff Mac-Duff picked up any clues since he arrived at the penthouse before daybreak this morning?

She longed to make out a suspect list and start piecing bits of information together. If only Ike were interested in this case. Even though they'd be leaving Lorenzo's tomorrow afternoon, they could have a great time trying to ferret out who drowned Buford Doakes, or at least come up with something to help the sheriff. She suppressed a sigh. She couldn't do it without Ike.

Ike's voice came into her thoughts. "When Ralph and I decided to drive up here, all we wanted to do was make sure you were okay and get you home," he said.

"But after hearing what happened to you, the situation changed," Ralph said.

"Right," Ike replied. "Sheriff MacDuff said he's calling in a detective tomorrow. Till the detective gets here, the sheriff will be going it alone on the investigation." He paused, looking into Liz's eyes. "I'm going to offer him my help."

Chapter Nine

Liz's heart bounded. She hadn't believed that Ike would want to get involved in a case for so brief a time, when chances were he'd have to leave it unsolved. But he was a first-rate detective. In the short time he'd spend helping the sheriff he'd be sure to come up with something leading to the solution of the case.

She knew Ike would welcome her input. He'd told her more than once that she was a wiz at latching onto clues. And Sophie would be a big help, too.

But moments later she had misgivings. Again, she wondered if the sheriff's reaction to Ike's offer would be negative. MacDuff seemed affable, but would he take Ike's offer of help to mean Ike regarded him as a hick lawman, incapable of handling a high profile murder case? Would he say he didn't need assistance from a hotshot New York detective?

Ike must have had an inkling of what was passing through her mind. "Don't worry about the sheriff pegging me as a NYPD know-it-all," he said. "That's not going to happen."

When Liz and Sophie exchanged puzzled glances, he laughed. "Ralph, shall we tell them how we managed to get through the roadblock?" he asked.

"I think the time's right," Ralph replied.

Ike turned to Liz. "Remember I told you I had something

to ask you when I called you back and couldn't get through to Sophie's phone?"

"Yes," Liz replied. "By the time you tried her phone, we were in the cave. What did you want to ask me?"

"I wanted you to find out the sheriff's first name. You'd already told me his last name's MacDuff. I got to thinking about it and wondering if he could be a member of the Mac-Duff family, friends of my grandparents."

"I remember you told me your grandparents lived on a farm near here. I'm sorry I couldn't help you out with the sheriff's first name."

"That's okay. I got it from the desk clerk. He told me it's Andy."

"And is Sheriff Andy MacDuff a member of the family your grandparents knew?"

Ike smiled. "Better than that. Andy and I were summertime pals when we were kids." He glanced out the window. "We used to go fishing in this lake."

"I get the picture," Liz said. "You got in touch with him and told him his old fishing buddy was planning to drive up to Lorenzo's today. I'll bet he was delighted to hear from you."

"He was. We figured it must be close to seventeen years since my last summer at the farm. My grandfather died when I was twelve and Grandma sold the old place and went to live with one of my aunts. He sounded like the same old Andy. We did a little reminiscing and it was like we were kids again."

"Did you tell him *you* were in police work, too?"

"Sure, and he reminded me how we used to play cops and robbers with a bunch of other kids, and I always wanted to be a robber. We had a good laugh about that."

"Sounds like you picked up where you left off years ago," Liz said, with a smile. It also sounded as if MacDuff wouldn't resent his old friend's offer to help in the investigation.

"Right, and I told him I'd heard about the homicide and asked if there'd be any problem getting into Lorenzo's today. I told him another officer was coming with me and we were planning to meet up with our girlfriends at the inn. I didn't mention we were concerned about you. Ralph and I figured he had enough on his mind without that. Andy took my vehicle data and said he'd notify the troopers to let us pass through."

"With you and MacDuff old buddies, he'll welcome your help," Sophie said.

"I think he will," Ike replied. "He told me he's had detective training but his deputies haven't. For a case as big as this he's sending for help, tomorrow, from the police department in Stroutsboro. He also mentioned contacting a P.I. friend."

"Sophie and I will be able to help, too," Liz said. "We didn't get around to telling you yet, but we were invited to Buford's party last night and we went."

"Is there anything else you haven't gotten around to telling us?" Ike growled. An instant later his face broke into a wry smile. "Well, I'd have been surprised if you'd declined."

"Yeah," Ralph said. "What normal, red-blooded woman would pass up the chance to share a hot tub with the biggest country rock star since Elvis?"

"This woman, for one, and Liz, too," Sophie replied. "We didn't get into the hot tub. We split during the photo session. Maybe that makes us abnormal and not very red-blooded."

Ralph flashed her a smile. "Sophie, my love, you're normal and red-blooded enough for me."

Knowing that Ike lacked Ralph's flair for compliments, Liz was content with a glance and a muttered, "you too, Liz."

This was immediately followed by, "since you two were present at the eventual crime scene, you must have observed a thing or two. I'm sure Andy will welcome any information you have."

"We picked up some interesting tidbits, didn't we Sophie?" Liz asked.

"Very interesting," Sophie replied.

Liz got the feeling that Sophie's heart was not totally into working on the Buford Doakes murder case. She wanted to get in some romantic time with Ralph.

A little of that with Ike would be nice, Liz thought, but delving into this case with him took priority. It was strange, but true, that sorting out suspects together, tossing ideas around and pouncing on clues was a big part of their mutual attraction.

"After dinner I want a rundown of those interesting *tid-bits*," Ike said, with a grin. "Also a list of people at the hot tub party you think might qualify as suspects."

At that moment the Lexus quartette entered the dining room. As they exchanged smiles and waves with Liz and Sophie, Liz also detected curiosity on their faces. Of course they'd be wondering who Ike and Ralph were, she decided.

"I take it you got acquainted with those men," Ike said.

"Yes. Nice guys. They're here on a golfing weekend," Liz replied.

"One of them's the man who offered to help us look for you," Ike said. "He approached us in the lobby while we were telling the sheriff you were missing."

"Oh?" Liz looked over at the table where Walt, Larry, Dennis and Jim were seated. "Which one?"

"The dark-haired one," Ike replied.

That would be Larry, Liz thought. Why had he been the only one of the four to offer help in searching for them?

When Ike continued, her question was answered. "He told us he and his friends had come back from a round of golf this afternoon, and his friends had gone up to their rooms. He'd stayed behind to look around in the gift shop and he overheard us talking to the sheriff about you."

Something Ike had said previously now flashed back into Liz's mind. *He checked out the lower part of the trail while Ralph and I hit the upper part.*

She also recalled thinking the young man who'd assisted in the search must have walked right past the icehouse cave, virtually hidden in the patch of woods. She'd decided he'd called their names, but they didn't hear him because that was while they were asleep. Now she asked herself, if someone had called out while walking near the cave, wouldn't they have awakened?

Lingering thoughts concerning Larry's hatred of Buford Doakes rushed to the forefront of her mind, and with them a host of questions and speculations. Was Larry's intense hatred for Buford a strong enough motive for murder? If Pedro had spread the word that Sophie was a cop, perhaps Larry assumed *she* was a cop, too. Perhaps Pedro had told Larry that she and Sophie were both New York City detectives. Did Larry want them out of the way so they couldn't help the sheriff with the interviews? Had he offered to search the lower trail to make sure nobody else did?

But it didn't add up. If Larry had followed them on their hike, what did he intend to do to keep them from helping the sheriff in his interrogations? He could not have anticipated that they'd go into the old icehouse and he could lock them in. Until she had some answers, she couldn't seriously consider Larry a suspect.

"Liz, you're very quiet all of a sudden," Ike said. His voice took on a teasing note. "Does that mean you've already come up with a suspect?"

"Maybe," Liz replied. "I'll run it by you after dinner."

"I have one suspect in mind already," Sophie said.

Sophie couldn't be thinking about Larry, Liz thought. She hadn't told her about Larry's hatred for Buford Doakes. Sophie was probably thinking about Ms. Frizzy Hair, she decided. Well, that wasn't farfetched. Buford's womanizing might have aroused his hometown girlfriend's jealousy to the boiling point.

"Where are we going to hold this post-dinner strategy session?" Ralph asked. "It has to be someplace where we can talk freely without being overheard."

"Your place or ours?" Sophie asked, with a grin.

"We'd be more comfortable in our suite," Ike said.

"You have a suite!" Liz and Sophie chorused.

"That must have set you back plenty," Sophie said. "How come you didn't just get regular rooms?"

"I'm surprised you were able to get *anything*," Liz said. "With Buford's concert scheduled for tonight, I'm sure the inn was booked solid."

"It was," Ralph replied. "But some of the fans weren't coming in till today. Those who heard about Buford in time, cancelled. The rest weren't able to get through the roadblock."

"The manager was glad we showed up," Ike said. "We got the suite for not much more than regular rooms."

When they finished their meal, Ike suggested they go directly to the suite. "We can get right to work discussing the case," he said. "When I see Andy tomorrow morning I'll tell him I want to help him, and if he's agreeable, I'll have some ideas for him."

Sophie glanced out the window. "Didn't any of you notice the moon?" she asked. "It's almost full . . ."

Sophie wanted to go out on the verandah and view the lake by moonlight, with Ralph, Liz thought. "Why don't you and Ralph check out the moon?" she asked. "You can meet us in the suite after awhile."

Sophie shot her a grateful grin. "Okay, we'll see you later."

"We'll try not to be too long," Ralph added.

He and Sophie headed for the French doors leading from the dining room onto the verandah.

As Liz and Ike walked through the dining room toward the lobby, they passed near the table where the Lexus four were seated. Liz glanced at them on the pretext of giving them a friendly smile, but her real purpose was to get a good look at Larry's face. Anyone who'd locked two young women in a secluded cave earlier in the day and then pretended to help search for them, might not yet be over the shock of seeing those same two women in the dining room. If Larry were the one who'd locked them in, surely he'd show some signs of surprise and disbelief.

She had only a moment to size up the situation, but that was enough to tell her that the expression on Larry's face looked no different from the others. Was Larry's a poker face?

"It's a good thing Ralph and I showed up here," Ike said, guiding her across the lobby to the elevators. "Those guys are interested in you and Sophie."

"But we're not interested in them," she retorted. That

wasn't entirely true. She was interested in Larry—if her suspicion could be called interest.

While they waited for the elevator they were surprised to see Sheriff MacDuff entering the lobby from the parking area.

"I thought you said he wasn't coming back to the inn till morning," Liz said.

"That's what he told me," Ike replied.

At that moment the sheriff spotted them and approached them. Though he was smiling as he greeted them, Liz noticed his round face looked drawn with fatigue. "You didn't expect to run into me again till tomorrow, did you, Ike?" he asked.

"No. I'm surprised. I thought you'd get a good dinner under your belt and head for some solid sack time," Ike said. "What brings you back here so soon?"

"I had the dinner all right, and a short nap," MacDuff replied. "But with this case on my mind, I couldn't stay asleep." He paused. "I got to thinking—I know you're leaving tomorrow, Ike, but would you consider helping me sort things out till the Stroutsboro detective gets here and my P.I. starts working?"

Liz could almost feel Ike's enthusiasm. "Sure, Andy."

MacDuff gave a grateful smile. "Thanks. I thought if you and I could discuss what I have so far, we might come up with something."

"If you're saying two heads are better than one, I have a better plan," Ike said. "How about five heads?"

It took MacDuff only a few seconds to assimilate this. "You're talking about your friend, Officer Perillo, and the young woman cop, and . . ." He looked at Liz. She saw doubt in his eyes. "I know your father's a retired homicide detective," he said. "But—"

Ike broke in. "Let me tell you about Liz Rooney. She's been following homicides since she was a kid, and she's developed a talent for digging up clues. For the past several months she's come up with angles that have helped me solve some tough cases. The DA knows about it and I haven't been bumped down to patrolling the Bronx, yet."

His lavish praise surprised Liz so much that she barely heard MacDuff saying the recommendation was good enough for him.

"Let's go up to my quarters, Andy," Ike continued. "Officers Perillo and Pulaski will join us there."

Getting on the elevator, the sheriff turned to Liz. "I heard you and Officer Pulaski took a very long hike today. You had your boyfriends thinking something had happened to you."

Ike looked at Liz. "You might as well tell him now," he said. "That way we won't have to brief him before we start discussing the case."

MacDuff shot Liz a keen glance. "What happened?"

By the time the elevator reached Ike's floor, Liz had described their ordeal. She watched a grim look come over the sheriff's face.

"There's no doubt in my mind, this ties in with the murder," he said, as the elevator doors slid open. "Have you told anyone else about it?"

"No, only the five of us know," Liz replied. "And whoever did it, of course."

"Good," MacDuff said. "Let's keep it that way."

This rural sheriff was no dummy, Liz thought. He didn't need Ike to tell him that the only other person who knew they'd been locked in the cave might get careless and drop a remark about it.

As they stepped off the elevator, the suggestion of a smile softened MacDuff's grim look. He turned to Ike. "Funny how things turn out," he said. "If you and Officer Perillo hadn't been worried about your girlfriends, you wouldn't have shown up here. Who'd ever think we'd be reunited after seventeen years, both of us cops, and working together on a case?"

Ike smiled. "I guess this takes us both back to when we were kids playing Cops and Robbers, except now I'm one of the good guys."

MacDuff gave a chuckle. "Yeah. Lucky for me that somewhere in those seventeen years you decided to get on the right side of the law."

Chapter Ten

"Wow—you guys are really traveling first class!" Liz exclaimed, as they entered Ike and Ralph's suite. Besides having a view of the lake, it had a sizeable living area furnished with a couch, a big, round coffee table, several comfortable-looking chairs and a large screen TV. A bar with beverage glasses, mugs and a coffee maker occupied one corner.

"Sorry, no hot tub," Ike said.

"No piano, either," MacDuff added. "The penthouse suite is the only one with a piano."

Just as Liz asked herself how a rural county sheriff would be familiar with the furnishings of a resort like Lorenzo's, he added, "I got that from Pedro, the bellman."

Pedro seemed to know everything, she thought. "Did he tell you who else besides Buford occupied the penthouse suite?" she asked.

"I managed to find that out myself," MacDuff replied with a grin. "All Buford's people, except the bodyguards, have rooms on lower floors. The penthouse suite has two double bedrooms—one for the guards, the other for Buford and his wife."

His wife! Liz stared at MacDuff in surprise. "I had no idea he was married," Liz said.

"You must have seen her at the party," MacDuff said. "Small blond woman."

So, Ms. Frizzy Hair is Mrs. Buford Doakes!

"According to Sid Kohner, his manager, it was a secret marriage, entered into when young girls first started getting the hots for Buford," MacDuff replied. "Keeping it secret was Buford's idea. He wanted his female fans to go on thinking he was single."

That explained Ms. Frizzy Hair's attitude, Liz thought. Under the circumstances, what wife wouldn't be sour? Wives had been known to kill husbands for less.

Ike's next comment seemed to tie in with her thoughts. "I guess the wife's high on your suspect list, Andy."

MacDuff nodded. "You guessed right."

The sound of a key in the door announced the arrival of Sophie and Ralph. Now they could get down to a serious discussion, Liz thought.

Briefing Sophie and Ralph about Buford's surprise marital status didn't take long.

"The more I find out about Buford the more disgusted I get," Ralph said.

"I think the wife did it. She finally had enough," Sophie added. "She seemed ready to explode when we saw her. Remember, Liz?"

"Right, she did," Liz replied. Still, she couldn't believe a woman as frail-looking as Ms. Frizzy Hair could have managed to drown a man over six feet tall and probably weighing one hundred eighty-five pounds.

They all sat down around the coffee table, ready to swap ideas.

"Let's start with possible suspects," MacDuff said. "I've eliminated almost everyone who wasn't in the penthouse last night. That includes guests who weren't at the party. I've given the okay for them to leave tomorrow, if they want to. And I think we can forget about Buford's manager as a possible suspect. Buford was a gold mine for him."

As a skilled arranger, Erwin Sporn must be getting a hefty salary from Buford, Liz thought. And after his wonderful arrangement of Buford's hit song, "True Blue Texas Love," maybe he got a raise. "Couldn't Erwin Sporn be ruled out too?" she asked.

MacDuff looked thoughtful. "Probably. According to what Sporn and Kohner told me, they left the party together around midnight. The bodyguards backed this up."

"What about others in Buford's entourage, like camera-men and musicians?"

"The guards said they all left soon after Kohner and Sporn, and my men didn't pick up on any beefs about Bu-ford during the interviews."

"I suppose the door to the suite was kept locked when a guard wasn't out there by the elevators," Sophie said. "No-body could get into the penthouse after the guards went to bed."

"Not unless he had a key," MacDuff said. "Kohner told me he had one—but like I said, he was making big dough off Buford. Why would he want him dead?"

"The inn staff, like housekeeping, would have access to keys," Sophie said.

"My men interviewed all staff people who'd have legiti-mate access to keys. No reason to connect any of them with the crime," the sheriff replied. "That includes the inn man-ager. He lives in a house on the grounds and, according to him and his wife and kids, he was there all night."

A person entering the penthouse elevator would first have to cross the lobby and pass right by the registration desk, Liz thought. "And the night clerk didn't see anyone getting on the private elevator after the party broke up?" she asked.

"He said he didn't," MacDuff replied. "But he admitted he took a couple of breaks. He went out onto the verandah for a smoke at two-thirty, he said, and again around three-thirty."

"The killer could have gone up there and come back down during those breaks," Ralph said. "With plenty of time in between."

Sophie shook her head. "That's a long shot. I still believe the killer has to be someone who slept in the penthouse last night."

Liz felt sure she was thinking about Mrs. Frizzy Hair Doakes. "Maybe not, Sophie," she said. "Maybe you're right and it wasn't someone who got hold of a key and sneaked back to the penthouse after the party was over, but remember, we talked about someone hiding there after the party ended, and attacking Buford when he came out of his room for another drink and another dip in the hot tub?"

"I remember now," Sophie replied. "We talked about that with Gail. It's a possibility, of course."

"Gail's a young woman we met at the party," Liz explained. "She was the only one besides us who didn't jump into a bikini and into the hot tub with Buford."

The sheriff scanned a couple of pages in his notebook. "Gail—here she is. When I interviewed her she told me she came here with three other women on a tennis weekend. She said she didn't leave the party till after one o'clock. She had some trouble getting one of her friends away from Buford."

"Yes, she told us about it," Sophie replied. "She said she was only able to get her friend away from him when he was distracted for a few minutes by a blond woman. And we all know, now, who that blond woman is. As far as I'm concerned, the jealous wife is the number one suspect."

"The wife's name is Bonnie Lou," MacDuff said. "When I interviewed her she seemed dazed—like she couldn't believe what happened. She told me she and Buford went to their room soon after the party broke up, and the guards went to theirs. But Buford didn't go to bed, she said. Instead, after a few minutes in the room, he told her he was going for another drink. He had an idea for a new song, he told her, and he wanted to think about it."

"I can't imagine how he could think straight after all that partying," Liz said. *And he didn't even take off his diamond-banded Stetson*, she thought. She recalled it had been found floating in the hot tub.

"I suppose Bonnie Lou claimed she went right to sleep and never heard a thing," Sophie said, in a scoffing tone.

MacDuff nodded. "She's a sound sleeper, she said. She told me the next thing she knew one of the guards was waking her up. He'd been asleep for a couple of hours when he awoke suddenly and noticed light coming from the hot tub area. He knew he'd turned all the lights off before everyone in the penthouse retired, so he went to investigate and found Buford submerged in the tub. He and the other guard got him out and called 911 but he was already dead."

Liz recalled the sheriff saying there'd been evidence of a struggle at the crime scene. One plant was standing a short distance away from the others, as if it had been knocked over, then picked up. "Whoever picked up the plant had to be Buford or the killer," she said. "I can't see Buford doing that, in his spaced out condition."

"Spaced out or not, most men wouldn't have bothered to pick it up," Sophie replied. "A woman would be more likely to do that. I think whoever was in the scuffle with Buford when the plant was knocked over was a woman, and I think that woman was Bonnie Lou, the jealous wife."

Liz had to admit that made sense. "Bonnie Lou had a stronger motive than jealousy," she added. "Buford wouldn't acknowledge her as his wife. It must have been tough, having to watch groupies swarm all over him, thinking he was an eligible bachelor. Maybe she'd reached the breaking point."

The sheriff jotted something in his notebook and studied the pages for a few moments. "Getting back to the tennis player," he said. "When I interviewed the guards, each of them told me this Gail had words with Buford while she was trying to coax her friend out of the hot tub."

"Of course he'd give her an argument," Sophie said.

"That wasn't all he gave her," MacDuff replied. "The guards heard him deliver a racial slur."

Liz felt stunned. Buford plunged to a new low in her estimation. But she couldn't believe the insult would turn an intelligent woman like Gail into a killer.

Sophie must have had the same reaction. "I don't buy that as a motive," she said. "Besides, didn't the guards see Gail leave the party with her friend?"

"They did," MacDuff replied.

"She could have gotten a key and returned. Let's keep her on the list," Ike said.

Liz knew she had to mention her suspicions about Larry. "I have something to tell you concerning the young man you said helped look for us on the trail," she said. She related Walt's story about Larry's hatred for Buford.

MacDuff put it all down in his notebook. "You say one of his friends told you this?" he asked.

"Yes, the one named Walt."

The sheriff consulted his notes. "Walt—yup. He didn't mention it when I interviewed him. He might have been covering for his friend. I'll do a follow-up on him tomorrow and see what he has to say about it. I'll question Larry again, too."

"I'm not defending Larry, but he didn't have a key," Liz said.

"Like Gail, it's possible he could have gotten one," Ralph said.

Ike looked around the group. "Let's sum up what we have on motives and opportunity."

Sophie jumped right in. "Bonnie Lou had both motive and opportunity."

"Larry had motive, all right," Liz said. "When you talk to him and Walt tomorrow, Sheriff, you'll find out if it was strong enough to make him want to kill. And Ralph's right. It's possible Larry could have gotten hold of a key."

"Gail's my number one suspect," Ralph said. "The stress of trying to get her friend to leave the party, and on top of that, the racial slur, could have added up to a need to get even. Let's say she got a key somehow and sneaked back to the penthouse. Maybe she didn't intend to kill him—just confront him and maybe slap his face."

Ike nodded. "By that time he might have been coming down from his high. A strong tennis swing could have stunned him and knocked him off balance."

"If the sides of the hot tub aren't very high and if they were standing near it when she slapped him, he could have fallen in," Ralph suggested.

"Or maybe she deliberately pushed him in," Liz said.

"He didn't fall into the water and he wasn't pushed," Mac-Duff said. "The location and position of the body indicated he'd gotten into the tub on his own. But there's no doubt someone hit him during a brief altercation *before* he got into the tub. There were red marks on his face."

Those red facial marks could have been the key to the killer's identity if Buford hadn't been submerged in the water, Liz thought. Too bad prints couldn't be lifted from wet skin.

"If he didn't fall into the water, then how did he drown?" she asked.

"Were there any red marks elsewhere on the body?" Ike asked.

"Yes—on his ankles," MacDuff replied. "I figured that's how he was drowned."

"Pulled under by the ankles?" Liz asked.

"Right—and held in that position," MacDuff replied.

"That kind of maneuver renders a victim helpless," Ike added.

Liz pictured Buford getting into the hot tub after Gail slapped him and Gail, still angry, reaching into the tub, grabbing his ankles and pulling him underwater. But, even though Buford was probably groggy when Gail slapped him, wouldn't he have socked her before getting into the tub?

"Seems to me if anyone slapped or punched him, he'd have struck back," Liz said. "But when we saw Gail in the dining room the next morning, she didn't look as if she'd been in a fight, did she, Sophie?"

Sophie shook her head. "Not a mark on her. What did Bonnie Lou's face look like this morning?"

"No noticeable marks," the sheriff replied. "But unlike Gail, she's heavy on the make-up."

"So, for suspects we have Gail, Larry, and Bonnie Lou," Sophie said.

Ike frowned. "I'm having second thoughts. At this stage of the game we shouldn't rule out *anyone* who was in the penthouse last night. That includes the bodyguards."

Ralph nodded in agreement. "If the scuffle between Buford and the killer didn't make enough noise to wake the guards up, you'd think the plant being knocked over would have. What do you know about them, Andy?"

"They're both old Texas pals of Buford's he's known for years," MacDuff replied. "But I'll have my P.I. run an intensive background check on them, anyway, first thing tomorrow." He paused. "Maybe we shouldn't write off Kohner and Sporn, either."

"Right, we shouldn't," Ike replied. "You never know. One of them might have had a motive strong enough to overcome the almighty dollar."

A sudden unrelated thought flashed into Liz's mind. "Whoever locked us in the cave would have left fingerprints on the stick when he put it back in the hasp."

"Yeah, but whichever one of you took the stick out of the hasp—her prints would be on it, too," Ike said.

Liz knew he was saying the blurred combination of prints would be impossible to lift accurately.

"Anyway," Sophie said, "whoever locked us in there might know by now that we got out. Maybe whoever did it has already gone to the cave and wiped off the stick and the hasp."

Liz visualized the killer, still a shadowy unidentified figure in her mind, sneaking along the dark trail to the cave by flashlight. She thought of the rock she'd placed against the door to keep it from swinging shut while they were inside. The rock was not very big. When the killer closed the door to lock them in, he might not have bothered to pick it up. The rock might have been pushed along by the door when he closed it.

She suggested this, adding, "My prints might be the only ones on the rock."

A chorus of voices replied to her suggestion. "Prints can't be lifted off rocks."

"I feel like a dummy," she said. "Am I the only one who didn't know that?"

"That might be the one thing your pop didn't tell you," Ike replied with a grin.

MacDuff gave him a questioning look. "Ike, about tomorrow's follow-up interviews—would you be willing to help me with them?"

"Sure," Ike said. "I'll pitch in till your detective arrives."

MacDuff smiled his thanks. "In the meantime, let's see what we have and determine who's going to be interviewed again tomorrow, and why."

They went over the list of suspects and possible motives. After more than an hour of this, Liz, Sophie and Ralph were all calling the sheriff by his first name, and he was doing the same with them.

"Andy, you have a busy day ahead, tomorrow," Liz said. "Interviews with Bonnie Lou, Gail, Larry, Walt, the bodyguards, Kohner, and Sporn."

"Not only that, but I've put out the okay for the news media," MacDuff replied. "This place will be overrun with reporters and TV cameras."

"Good thing you're sending for a detective tomorrow," Sophie said.

"I've decided not to send for him till after you folks leave," MacDuff replied. "Till then, I have all the help I need. Is that okay with all of you?"

The okay was unanimous. They all thanked him, saying they'd do everything they could. But even with Ike at the helm, the time frame seemed too short for them to sail into a prime suspect, Liz thought. And her own sleuthing hadn't been much help so far. Larry's hatred of Buford was the closest thing to a clue she'd come up with.

"At first I thought of taking you all to the crime scene tomorrow," MacDuff said. "But my interviews could last all morning and you'll be leaving in the afternoon. I think we should go up there tonight."

A tingle of anticipation swept over Liz. This was unexpected. She'd thought Ike would be the only one allowed at the crime scene. She felt energized by the prospect of going back to the penthouse and recreating Buford's drowning in her mind. She knew she was good at picking up clues at crime scenes.

"Okay," Ike said. "We've pretty well covered motives, but before we go up to the penthouse, we should go over each suspect in depth. Did any one of them say or do anything we haven't discussed? We need to concentrate on each one."

Sophie glanced at her watch. "It's been awhile since dinner. I need something to keep me going. At least a cup of coffee."

"No problem." Ike said, getting to his feet and heading for the bar. "Coffee all around?" he asked.

Just as he spoke, a knock sounded on the door, and a voice, "Room service." Liz thought the voice sounded familiar.

"They must have gotten the wrong room number," Ike said, on his way to the door. "We didn't order anything from room service, did we?"

"No, but I wish we had," Sophie replied. "I don't know about the rest of you, but I'm going to need something besides coffee before we break up for the night."

Ike opened the door. Standing there next to a room service cart with a large covered platter on it was Pedro.

Chapter Eleven

"Allo," Pedro said, with a toothy smile. "I got big pizza pie for you."

While Sophie exclaimed "oh, good!" Ike shook his head. "We didn't order anything, Pedro."

"Better check the room number." Ralph added.

"I just deliver to room down hall and I got one extra pizza on cart," Pedro explained. "I know you having meeting in here so I think maybe you like something to eat."

The idea of pizza straight from Lorenzo's ovens made Liz forget she'd put away a steak dinner less than three hours ago. She was about to say so, when Sophie's voice rang out.

"Bring it in!"

Ike hesitated a moment before stepping aside to let Pedro wheel in the cart.

The unmistakable aroma of freshly baked pizza pie sent Sophie rushing to lift the platter cover. She gazed at the large pie. "Wow, twelve slices," she said, "half sausage and cheese and half pepperoni and a lot of other stuff. Thanks for thinking of us, Pedro."

"Yeah, thanks," Ike said, digging into his pocket for a tip.

"I know you got coffee in here. You need anything else?" Pedro asked.

"This will be enough, thanks," Ike replied. "How did you know a meeting was being held in here this evening?"

Pedro looked at Sophie. "I was in lobby near elevator and I hear you and the other police talking about meeting," he said. "I watch what floor you get off and I remember the two police from New York have this room."

Nothing much got by Pedro, Liz thought. "So, when you found you had an extra pizza aboard, you decided we might like it," Liz said.

"And you were right," Sophie said. She'd already taken plates and paper napkins out of a cabinet.

"Well, I go now," Pedro said. "You enjoy."

He'd barely closed the door when Ike put the cover back on the pizza platter and gave them all a questioning glance. "Before we dig into this, am I the only one who thinks there's something fishy here?"

"I'm with you, Ike, and it's not the anchovies," MacDuff replied.

"Me, too," Ralph added. "Pedro showing up here is too much of a coincidence."

Sophie frowned. "What are you suggesting?"

"It's possible Pedro wanted to find out who was at this meeting," Ike replied.

"So what?" Liz asked. "He likes to find out as much as he can about the guests and what they're up to. He's just one of those nosy people who has to be in the know about everything."

"He's also the only one not on our suspect list who was in the penthouse the night of the murder," Ike replied.

Sophie answered in a peevish tone. "So put him on the list and let's eat—unless you think the pizza is poisoned."

"No, I don't think it's poisoned," Ike said with a laugh. "But we shouldn't overlook anything that looks suspicious, no matter how unrelated to the crime it appears to be."

Liz recalled Pop telling her this. He'd also advised her not to totally disregard her flights of imagination. Okay, Pop, she said to herself, here's something highly imaginative— Pedro could be in cahoots with the killer and acting as a spy.

Aloud, she said, "Pedro might have a connection to the killer."

Evidently Ike and the sheriff thought more of this possibility than she did. They both nodded.

"I won't wait till tomorrow to contact my P.I. friend," Mac-Duff said. "I'll get in touch with him tonight. That way he can get an early start tomorrow, checking out the guards and finding a possible link between Pedro and one of the suspects."

"If Pedro is Mexican, maybe he's from Texas," Ralph said. "He might have a link to one of the bodyguards."

"If there's a connection, this P.I. will find it," MacDuff said. "He's a former Pittsburgh investigator, tops in his line. He has sources in every field. After he's gone into the guards' backgrounds and Pedro's, we'll know a lot more."

"Now can we eat?" Sophie asked.

An hour or so later, MacDuff had contacted his P.I., the pizza was long gone and they'd discussed all the suspects. Now they were ready for the crime scene.

They took the elevator down to the lobby. Liz looked around to see if Pedro might be lurking about, but there was no sign of him.

The sheriff lowered the police barricade tape stretched across the door to the penthouse elevator. "Nobody but me and my men have been up there since early this morning," he said. "The bodyguards and Bonnie Lou moved down to other rooms. I had the door to the suite padlocked, and I have the only key."

"Good move," Ike said.

"It was the only way we could keep the crime scene secure," MacDuff replied. "We don't have the manpower big cities have. Matter of fact, we don't have the homicides, either. The last murder that happened out here was almost a year ago. A fight in the parking lot of a Bucksville bar." He grinned at Ike. "I didn't need any help with that one."

"You're doing great with this one, Andy," Ike replied. "You came up with some damn strong leads for us to go on and you have your private investigator working on it, too. Before we pull out tomorrow, we should have a prime suspect."

* * *

On the elevator, Liz felt the familiar feeling of excitement. Though she'd gone to numerous crime scenes with her boss, the medical examiner, each new one always brought on this feeling. She never knew when she might stumble on something that would stimulate her imagination. Her wildfire imagination, Pop called it. More than once, it had led to a clue that helped Ike solve a case.

They stepped off the elevator into the penthouse foyer, dimly lit by an overhead fixture. Liz watched MacDuff open the padlocked door. What a difference a day made, she thought. When she and Sophie passed through that door last night, they could never have imagined the grim happening ahead.

MacDuff switched on lights, bringing the shadowed crime scene into view. Beyond a cluster of tall potted plants, palms and other varieties, the water in the hot tub glinted, eerily quiet.

Liz gazed at it. For a fleeting moment, she could almost see Buford, clad in swim trunks, wearing his diamond-banded Stetson, lolling in the water, reveling in the proximity of a dozen bikini-clad bodies.

She saw the plant MacDuff said had been knocked over and uprighted, most likely by the killer. As he'd said, it was standing apart from the others. It looked undamaged by the fall, and she noticed no soil had spilled out onto the floor. The soil level must be deep down in the container, well below the rim, she decided. Like the other containers, it was tall and made of what looked like cement, and studded all over with stones. Small rocks were imbedded in a rim that protruded around the top. The killer would have grabbed hold of the rim to pick it up, she thought.

Ike's voice came into her musings. "Andy, I don't see the famous diamond-banded Stetson. Did you decide to see if that felt fabric might hold some fingerprints?"

"Yes. I've never come across a fabric that held fingerprints, but I thought it was worth a try. The killer's hands might possibly have come in contact with it during the scuffle. If it held any prints, the crown area would be dry enough to lift them."

Of course Buford's prints would be on the hat, Liz thought. An additional set of liftable fingerprints on the black Stetson might well be the killer's.

"Before we sit down for another go-round on the suspects, I want to find out how much noise that plant made when it hit the floor," MacDuff said. "If Buford closed his bedroom door when he went out, Bonnie Lou might not have heard anything, but the guards would keep their door open. Ike, will you and Ralph go to their room? I'll knock over a plant. You can decide if the noise could wake the guards up."

"With the door open, it might," Liz said. "Those pots are heavy, and the stone insets all over them and those rocks around the rim make them even heavier."

"Liz, I noticed you didn't ask Andy if there were fingerprints on the toppled pot," Ike said. "How come?"

"I never make the same mistake twice," she replied. "Having been told by experts that prints can't be lifted from rocks, I figured the same goes for stones. Anyway, the killer would have picked up the pot by its rim, and that's all rocks."

Ike flashed her an approving look as he and Ralph headed for the guards' bedroom. "Do some talking while we're back there," he said. "And make it fairly loud."

MacDuff walked over to the containers arranged around the tub and selected a palm plant. In a voice loud enough to be heard in the bedrooms, he said. "I don't think that plant was knocked over accidentally, and here goes another one."

Sophie chimed in, "Tim—berrr!"

With a thud, the container landed midway between the carpet and the tile bordering the tub, and rolled a few inches. The plant was undamaged. Most of its fronds missed hitting the floor because of the container's protruding rim.

Ike and Ralph appeared a few moments later. "We heard something, but we agree it wouldn't have awakened either of us," Ike said.

"Did you hear my voice?" MacDuff asked.

"Yeah, and Sophie's too, but that wouldn't have brought anyone out of a sound sleep, either," Ralph replied.

"When I first sized up the scene, I wasn't sure if the guards or Bonnie Lou could have slept through what happened, but it looks like they did," MacDuff said.

"Maybe not," Sophie said. "Bonnie Lou claimed she went right to sleep after Buford left the bedroom, but she could have followed him out here and started complaining about him fooling around. One thing might have led to another and it got physical."

"Would a small woman like Bonnie Lou be strong enough to pull a big man underwater by the ankles and keep him there?" Liz asked.

"Sure," Sophie replied. "We both know bodies are weightless in water. And like Ike said before, with that kind of move, there's nothing a person can do to save himself from being drowned."

Liz thought about this for a moment. "You'd think he would have yelled and kicked."

"He wouldn't have had time to yell," Ike said. "He was submerged before he knew what was happening. And if the killer had a firm grip on his ankles, he couldn't have done enough kicking to break loose."

"And don't forget, Buford was not exactly in top form," Sophie replied.

Liz pictured Bonnie Lou crouching on the rim of the tub, reaching for Buford's ankles. Even for a man, or for tall, athletic Gail, this seemed awkward. For someone Bonnie's size and strength it seemed improbable. Wouldn't she have to get into the water to pull him under? Liz couldn't decide. MacDuff was unaccustomed to investigating baffling homicides, but he'd had some detective training. When he arrived at the crime scene, he would have picked up even the slightest trace of dampness on the carpet between the hot tub and Bonnie's bedroom.

Unless Bonnie dried herself off thoroughly after the deed was done. That would mean she brought along a towel— maybe even a dry nightgown, when she followed Buford out of their bedroom. It would also mean this wasn't a homicide resulting from a burst of pent-up anger. It would be premeditated murder.

But if all this had occurred to *her,* wouldn't MacDuff have thought of it, too? Wouldn't he have checked Bonnie's bathroom for wet clothing? And if he'd found anything suspicious, wouldn't he have let them know about it? The answer was yes to all.

Almost as if MacDuff guessed what she was thinking, he came out with a concurrent statement. "There were no signs that the killer got into the tub to pull Buford under. We believe Buford was reclining in the water with his feet near the surface when it happened. The guard who found him said the body was submerged in a corner of the tub. We're sure the killer knelt on the side of the tub and reached in and grabbed his ankles. My men checked this out."

A man would have a longer reach than petite Bonnie Lou, Liz thought. "Could a small woman have done it?" she asked. As she spoke, she glanced at Sophie. This was the first time they hadn't seen eye-to-eye on a suspect.

"Possibly," the sheriff replied.

"You want to check it out for yourself, Liz?" Ike asked, with a grin.

"I'll pass on the grounds that I didn't bring along any dry clothes," Liz said. She went back to square one—the guards and Bonnie Lou, plus Gail, Larry, Kohner, and Sporn. How could Ike and the sheriff unravel this tangle of suspects by tomorrow afternoon?

"Let's go over motive and opportunity again," MacDuff said, leading the way to the sitting area.

"I'll go first," Sophie said, snuggling into an overstuffed armchair. "I still believe Bonnie Lou had the strongest motive, and she had more opportunity than anyone else."

"The guards certainly had the opportunity," Ike said. "But we won't know about motive till the background checks come in, tomorrow." He glanced at Liz. "You're right, thinking Larry's hatred of Buford makes a strong motive, but there's nothing to put him at the scene. Maybe after Andy questions him and his friend again, we'll know if he had the opportunity."

"Gail had motive," Ralph said. "And if she got hold of a key and came back to the penthouse to confront Buford about the racial slur, that would be her opportunity."

"That leaves Kohner and Sporn," Liz said. "Kohner had a key to the penthouse suite. That would give him the opportunity. But I can't think of any reason why he'd drown Buford. That would be like killing the goose who lays golden eggs."

"Again, we might find something out, tomorrow," Mac-Duff said. "As for Sporn, Buford wasn't exactly a golden goose for him, but anyone doing music arrangements for a big star is making good money."

"That seems to eliminate motive," Ike said.

"And he didn't have a key to the penthouse suite," Liz added. "That eliminates opportunity."

"Like Andy said, we might find something out tomorrow," Ike replied. "Till then, I guess that does it for the motives and opportunities."

"Oh!" Liz exclaimed. "We're forgetting Pedro again! I know you said you didn't consider him a suspect, Ike, but . . ."

Ike broke in. "I agree, he fits into the picture somewhere."

"Maybe he shouldn't be ruled out as a suspect," Liz said. "His motive could have been robbery. He might only have planned to swipe Buford's diamond hatband but things went wrong. And don't forget, he had access to room keys."

MacDuff gave an unexpected grin. "There's something I didn't get around to telling you. Kohner told me those diamonds on the hatband are fakes."

After a moment of stunned silence, Ralph was the first to speak. "Who else besides Kohner knew this?"

"According to him, only the guards and Bonnie Lou."

"As unlikely as it seems, we shouldn't rule Pedro out," Ike said. "This could have been a robbery gone wrong. For all we know he has a rap sheet a mile long."

MacDuff nodded. "There could be a Texas connection somewhere. We'll find out tomorrow."

"But even if it was a robbery gone wrong and Pedro didn't intend to kill Buford, wouldn't he have stolen the hatband, anyway?" Ralph asked.

"Not if he knew the stones aren't real," Liz replied.

"How would he know they were fakes?" Ralph asked.

Liz laughed. "Pedro knows everything," she joked. She glanced at Sophie, expecting her to put in her two cents worth. Sophie had only spoken once since settling into the cushy armchair. Now the reason for her silence was obvious. She was asleep.

"I think Sophie's trying to tell us something," Liz said.

Ralph smiled at the sight of his fiancée, out like a light. "Looks like it's time to break this up."

"We're about done anyway, aren't we, Andy?" Ike asked.

"Yes, we've gone as far as we can tonight," MacDuff replied. He looked around the group. "Thanks for your help. Ike and I will do the interviews in the manager's office tomorrow, after breakfast."

"They shouldn't take more than a couple of hours," Ike said. "Shall we all meet up here, say, eleven, to see what we have?"

"Yes," MacDuff replied. "By then I'll have the Texas background checks. They're in an earlier time zone out there. Our checks on Sid Kohner and Erwin Sporn will come in later in the day."

In time for an evaluation, Liz hoped. Again, she wondered if Ike could come up with anything to help his old friend, before heading back to Manhattan.

Ralph had woke up Sophie and was guiding her toward the door. "Ike, I'll see our ladies back to their room if you and Andy want to have a few final words," he said.

Liz looked at Ike, hoping he'd say he'd go with them. Before she went to sleep, she wanted to be hugged and kissed and told she was loved.

"Yeah, Ralph, thanks," Ike said. "I have some points I want to cover with Andy."

He walked to the door with them. Liz called good night to the sheriff, then turned to Ike. "Good night," she said, trying to keep the disappointment out of her voice.

"Good night, Liz," he replied. "I know you're tired. You had quite a day. I guess you won't feel like getting up for an early breakfast with me."

Before she could tell him she might, he added, "I'll see you in the penthouse at eleven."

The brush of his mouth on hers could barely be described as a kiss, but it was better than nothing.

Chapter Twelve

The next morning both Liz and Sophie were awakened by the sound of activity in the parking lot—voices, car doors slamming and vehicle engines starting.

"What's going on?" Sophie murmured. "And what time is it, anyway?"

Liz checked the digital clock on the nightstand. "Wow—quarter to eight," she replied. "I guess we were both wiped out after yesterday." She got out of bed and went to the window.

"Sophie, you have to see this to believe it," she said. "It's Forty-Second Street and Broadway out there."

Sophie yawned and burrowed into her pillow. "Andy told us he'd given the word for guests to leave this morning if they wanted to."

"It's more than that," Liz replied. "There's two-way bumper-to-bumper traffic on the road coming down to the inn and I see a couple of TV camera trucks."

"The news media's here!" Sophie threw off her covers, jumped out of bed and joined Liz at the window. "What a snarl-up," she said, looking down at departing guests packing their cars, a line of cars leaving and incoming vehicles jamming the road, waiting to get into the parking area.

"Look," Sophie said, "isn't that Pedro out there, directing traffic?"

Liz looked. "It certainly is."

They watched the ubiquitous bellman performing stop and go motions and leaning into vehicle windows, talking to drivers.

"I'll bet he's finding out who's who among the reporters and which newspapers and networks they represent," Sophie said.

"And he could be giving reporters an earful, too," Liz added. "You know how he likes to spread information around." She turned away from the window. "I hope Ike and Andy can get their interviews going before this whole place is crawling with reporters."

The phone rang at that moment and Sophie grabbed it.

She reported it was Ralph. Ike and Andy had started interviewing the possible suspects who'd had early breakfasts, contacting them as they came out of the dining room. "He said they've finished with Larry and Walt, and Gail's next."

"By the time they're done with those three, the other suspects will be in the dining room, and they can take it from there," Liz said. But the bereaved Bonnie Lou would call room service instead of going to the dining room, she decided. That probably held true for other members of Buford's entourage, as well. By now they must know the news media was on the scene. With reporters and photographers swarming the inn, Buford's people would want to avoid the inevitable frenzy of questions and cameras.

Sophie must have had the same thought. "Most likely Ike and Andy will have to interview the others in their rooms," she said.

Liz had an additional thought. "I guess we should get down to the dining room as quickly as we can. With all those news hounds crowding in, it'll be packed."

"Ralph mentioned that. He said he ate with Ike and Andy, but he'll save the table for us. He'll see us down there as soon as we can make it."

They showered and dressed in shorts and tee shirts. "Only six more hours and we'll be getting ready to leave," Liz said, as she dabbed on some lipstick. In that short span of time, would they be able to help Andy MacDuff at all? She'd grown to like Ike's boyhood friend. He was certainly not the bumbling hick lawman the killer evidently assumed he was. At their meeting in the penthouse later, she hoped each one of them could contribute a piece to the puzzle of Buford's drowning, and enough of the picture would emerge before they had to leave.

"I was wondering about something before I went to sleep last night," Sophie said, giving her hair a final fluff. "Does whoever locked us in the icehouse know that we got out? The only suspects we saw last night were Larry and Pedro."

"Neither one seemed surprised to see us, but you can bet Pedro has started spreading the word that the two hikers came back safe and sound," Liz said. "You can bet he told your number one suspect, Bonnie Lou. She's probably been calling room service for her meals, and Pedro would have made sure he was the one who delivered them."

"Yeah, he probably did," Sophie replied, as they left their room. "He seems to be everywhere, all the time, from early morning to late at night."

"Like he told us, he gets extra pay for working long hours," Liz said, while they walked to the elevator. "Besides, it gives him a chance to pursue his favorite pastime, finding out everything there is to know about the guests."

Sophie waited till they were on the elevator before replying. "Do you suppose he knows that Bonnie Lou was married to Buford? That's one thing he never told us."

"Maybe he didn't know it at the time, but the way he keeps his ears flapping, you can bet he'll pick up on it, if he hasn't already."

The elevator doors opened on a lobby crowded with a combined assembly of incoming news reporters and outgoing guests. The clerk at the registration desk looked harried. Liz noticed he wasn't the night clerk they'd seen earlier. That one was probably grabbing some sleep somewhere in the inn, she decided, as they made their way into the dining room. It, too, was filled. Ralph, waiting for them at a table, rose to greet them.

"Good morning," he said, giving them each a hug and Sophie a kiss. "Some mob out there."

"Yes, and in here, too," Sophie replied, glancing around. "If it weren't for you, we'd have to wait for a table."

"Thanks for keeping yours for us," Liz said, as they sat down.

"I'm starved," Sophie said, picking up a menu.

"Service is going to be slow," Ralph said. "Most of the inn staff live in town and the dining room's been short handed because of the roadblock. It didn't matter too much before the news media showed up, but now . . ."

"Isn't Andy allowing inn employees through yet?" Sophie asked.

"He is. The troopers got word to let them in along with the news media but some of them haven't shown up yet. They're probably caught in the traffic jam. The manager had to take over the registration desk."

A harried-looking young waitress, passing by with a full tray of food, paused to plunk a pot of coffee on their table. "I'll take your orders as soon as I can. Sorry. It's just me and one other," she added.

"Thanks. This will tide us over," Liz said, starting to fill their cups.

An angry male voice sounded from a nearby table. "Let's have some coffee over here."

They all turned to see a middle-aged man with thinning brown hair and a bulbous nose, sitting alone. The combination of his anger and his oversized nose gave him a distinctly unpleasant look.

"Yes sir, I'll bring it in a few minutes," the waitress replied, hurrying off with her tray.

"The party you just brought that pot of coffee to came in after I did," the irate man called after her.

"You're wrong about that," Ralph told him. "You came in while I was waiting for the ladies to join me, and I asked the waitress to bring coffee when she got the chance."

Liz summoned a smile. "Pass your cup over and I'll fill it."

The man looked somewhat placated. "Thanks," he muttered.

Liz sensed he was still in the mood to give the waitress a bad time. "They're very shorthanded this morning," she told him, returning his full cup. "The waitress is doing the best she can."

As she spoke she noticed he was wearing a press badge. Then she saw a small camera bag on the floor next to his chair. It wasn't only the poor dining room service that had him riled, she thought. With MacDuff busy interviewing, and most of the principals in the case in seclusion, there hadn't been a chance to get statements or photo shots.

"That Big-Schnoz guy's a reporter," she whispered to Sophie and Ralph. "He was probably one of the first to arrive and he expected to have all his material by this time."

"Too bad he didn't run into Pedro," Sophie replied.

At that moment the waitress paused at their table again. "Good news," she said. "We have a couple of pinch hitters. Someone's coming to take your breakfast orders, right now." Turning to the irate reporter, she added, "yours, too, sir."

Minutes later they heard a familiar voice. "Allo . . ."

Bellman, Room Service, Traffic Director and now Dining Room Waiter!

"Hello, Pedro," they chorused.

Pedro flourished a pencil above a notepad and eyed their menus. "You know what you like for breakfast?"

Liz looked at Sophie. "Let's get the Special. It'll probably be quick."

"Right," Sophie replied. "Two Specials, Pedro."

Bulbous Nose was not about to be left out. "I'll have the Special, too," he called.

"Three *Speciales*," Pedro said, writing it down. He nodded approval. "*Speciale* very good. I take one up to the *wiudo,* Señora Doakes this morning. She say she like it. She not eat all yesterday." He paused, unaware that his translation of *widow* was slightly off, and apparently relishing the notion that his reference to Buford's secret marriage would be big news.

Sophie wasted no time in letting him know this was no surprise to them. "How is Mrs. Doakes feeling this morning?" she asked.

Pedro covered his disappointment. "She still got shock, but she okay." He started toward the kitchen.

Bulbous Nose's voice drifted after him. "Hold it. Did I understand you to say Buford has a wife?"

Pedro beamed at him over his shoulder. "Sure, he married secret to girlfriend from Texas."

"His girlfriend? Bonnie Lou?" the reporter asked excitedly.

Pedro nodded. The reporter jumped to his feet. "I'm going out on the verandah," he said. "Bring my breakfast to the table. I'll be back in a few minutes."

They watched him rush out, pulling a phone from his pocket on the way.

"Well that blows the secret of Buford's marriage," Ralph said. "Half the dining room now knows about it, and that reporter got a big scoop for his paper."

"Maybe now he'll be in a better frame of mind," Liz replied.

The reporter was almost smiling when he returned from the verandah and lit into his waiting breakfast. While eating her Special Liz saw him hail Pedro, passing by with a tray for another table. Though he kept his voice low, Liz heard some of what he said.

"I want to talk to you . . ."

Evidently Pedro was agreeable and a meeting was set up. With an air of satisfaction, the reporter finished his breakfast and left the dining room.

"That newshound's going to pump Pedro for every drop of information he has," Sophie said.

Liz nodded. "I wonder what newspaper or network he's with."

"We'll know when the news about Buford's marriage breaks," Ralph replied. "The first newspaper or TV station to announce it will be that big-nosed guy's employer."

Liz looked at Sophie's empty plate and her own. "I guess we should go," she said, taking a final sip of coffee. "People are waiting for tables."

In the crowded lobby, guests were still lining up to check out. The groupies, a somber-looking bunch compared to Friday night's giggling gaggle, were going out the door to the parking area. More newspeople were streaming in.

Beyond the registration desk, adjacent to the penthouse elevator, she noticed a closed door. That must be the manager's office, she decided. Were Andy and Ike still in there or had they started interviewing the rest of the suspects in their rooms?

"We have almost two hours to kill before our meeting with Andy and Ike in the penthouse," Ralph said. "What would you two lovely ladies like to do?"

Liz knew without a doubt that Sophie and Ralph would like to spend some time alone. "Why don't you two go for a walk or something?" she asked. "I'll just nose around here by myself."

"I wouldn't feel right, leaving you on your own," Sophie said.

"Yeah," Ralph agreed. "Let's all go down to the dock and check out the boats. Maybe we could rent one."

Liz shook her head. "No. Really. I want to do some serious thinking before we go up to the penthouse." She also wanted to keep her eye on the door to the manager's office, in case Ike and Andy came out. She felt a strong need to see Ike, if only for a few minutes.

"Well, if you're sure . . ." Sophie said.

"I'm positive. I'll see you back here at quarter of eleven."

While she watched them cross the lobby, hand in hand, she decided to find out if Ike and Andy were still interviewing in the manager's office. She went to the registration desk, where the inn manager was still assuming the clerk's duties. She waited till he had a free moment.

"Is the sheriff still in your office?" she asked.

"No, ma'am," the manager replied. "He and the New York detective left there about half an hour ago. They're interviewing in some of the guests' rooms, now."

She held back a sigh. That meant she wouldn't see Ike till they met at the crime scene. And then of course they'd be with Andy, Sophie and Ralph. She longed for even a few minutes alone with him. He could have worked that out last night. They could have found some way to be alone. At the very least, they could have shared the first real kiss since he arrived. He seemed so distant last night.

A recollection of something Pop had told her nipped her self-pity in the bud. When he noticed that her friendship with Ike was deepening, he'd said she must understand that frequently, when a good detective was on a tough homicide case, he closed his mind to almost everything else.

"Your mother will back me up on that," Pop had said with a wry smile. "When we were first married there were times I was so preoccupied, she thought I didn't love her."

Feeling better, Liz walked around the lobby for awhile. She spent some time browsing in the gift shop before deciding to go out on the verandah. She'd find a chair, reflect on the development of the case, and enjoy the view.

She'd just settled down when she realized she wasn't alone out there. A man at the opposite end of the verandah was huddled in a chair, talking on a cell phone. A second look told her the man was the music arranger, Erwin Sporn. Obviously he wasn't aware of her presence or he wouldn't have continued his very audible and intimate conversation.

"Sweetheart, please be reasonable . . . how could I be enjoying myself after what happened . . . ? Anyway, this place is way out in the sticks . . . Darling, how many times have I told you, whether it's Vegas or a hick place like this, I miss you when I'm on tour. . . ."

Liz didn't know what else to do except give a discreet cough. Instantly, Sporn spun around. His face reddened. Without a word, he bolted out of his chair and hurried off the verandah into the lobby.

She recalled he'd been on the phone every time she'd seen him, and, though she hadn't heard any part of those conversations, he always seemed troubled. Now she asked herself if those frequent, troubled conversations could have been with a nagging girlfriend or wife, who resented his occasional tours with Buford and phoned him constantly to complain. Most likely she even accused him of playing around while he was on the road.

But Erwin Sporn didn't appear to be the two-timing type. The way he talked to this woman, whoever she was, indicated he was in love with her. She must be very self-centered, Liz thought. Apparently she hadn't phoned to offer empathy regarding Buford's drowning. Instead, she voiced the usual complaints. His attempts to placate her this time included reminders of his dislike for tours "way out in the sticks." She probably shared his disdain for "hick places." Sporn was henpecked, Liz decided.

At that moment she saw something on the floor near the chair the music arranger had so hastily vacated. It looked like a small notebook. She walked the length of the verandah and picked it up. It was a notebook, all right, dropped in his hurry to get away. She'd try to find him, right now, and return it to him. Maybe that would make up for her having overheard snippets of his conversation with his nagging wife or girlfriend.

After a thorough search of the crowded lobby, she didn't find Erwin Sporn. He must have gone up to his room, she decided. Okay, she'd take the notebook to the registration desk and turn it over to the manager. She was about to do that when a voice from behind startled her.

"I'd like to talk to you, Detective Rooney."

She recognized the voice. Even before she whirled around, she knew she'd be face-to-face with Bulbous Nose.

Chapter Thirteen

Detective Rooney! Of course that bit of erroneous information had come straight from Pedro. Her first impulse was to let this obnoxious reporter go on believing it. Deceiving him might be fun.

Bulbous Nose reached into the pocket of his dark green polyester slacks and took out a business card. "Cliff Yaker, *The National Informer*," he said, thrusting the card at her.

That sleazy tabloid! She ignored the card in his outstretched hand. If she said anything at all to him he'd snap her photo before she knew what was happening. She'd be on the front page of his scandal sheet. She could almost see the headline.

NYPD CHICK SHAMUS ON ROCK STAR MURDER CASE

What a stir that would make among Pop's former colleagues at the station house. They all knew Frank Rooney's daughter had been into murder cases since she was a kid, but now they'd think she was passing herself off as a homicide detective! She didn't even want to imagine Pop's reaction if he got wind of it down in Florida. And Ike. She pictured his face, scowling as he told her this time she'd gone too far—maybe even saying he'd have to distance himself from her. She must set this reporter straight.

"You're mistaken, Mr. Yaker," she began. "I'm not . . ."

He broke in, his eyes like twin brown beads, staring at her from either side of his oversized nose. "Are you denying you're part of a team of New York detectives brought in by the local sheriff?"

She felt her temper igniting. Where did this yellow rag journalist get off, talking to her like this? "I don't have to deny anything to you," she said. "I don't want your card. I'm not interested in talking to you."

As she turned and walked away, she realized she was still holding Erwin Sporn's notebook. She dropped it into her purse when she heard the tabloid reporter's voice close behind her. He wasn't fazed at all. No doubt he was accustomed to being brushed off, like some creepy insect.

"If you're trying to keep this under wraps, it won't work," he said, with a sneer. "I already have enough for a good story. The New York Police Commissioner doesn't know about the under-the-counter deal you and your detective pals have going with the local sheriff, does he?"

This sounded as if he planned to write a story about four NYPD detectives working out-of-state on the sly. Sort of an exposé of corruption in the ranks of the NYPD. It would be a good yarn if it were true. But truth was secondary to tabloids like the *Informer*—if they considered it at all. She had to shake this guy off.

"I told you I don't want to talk to you," she said. "Please leave me alone." She walked to a nearby chair and sat down. Yaker stood, watching her, as if he were deciding whether or not to keep following her.

She reviewed his remarks. He'd referred to Ike, Ralph and Sophie as her pals. This could mean he didn't know their names. But how did he know hers? After a few moments of thought she remembered the name tag on her luggage. Sophie didn't have one on the bag she'd brought along. Evidently, neither did Ike and Ralph, or Pedro would have passed along all their names. When Pedro saw Ike and Ralph talking to the sheriff on their arrival, he probably hung around and listened. That's how he found out Ike was a

NYPD detective and Ralph an officer. Like all gossip, the facts were garbled, and now all four of them had emerged as NYPD detectives.

Tabloid reporter Yaker had decided to proceed with his efforts to talk with her. He found a nearby chair and drew it close to hers. "Aw, come on. It doesn't have to be like this," he cajoled. "A little cooperation and I can slant the story and have *you* come out smelling like a rose."

He wanted to make a deal in exchange for the names of her "pals."

Ike loved to remind her of her quick temper. Her red-haired Irish temper, he called it. If he could have seen her at that moment she'd be in for plenty of teasing. She jumped out of her chair, exclaiming, "I told you I don't want to talk to you! Quit following me around, you scandal sheet jerk."

Her voice carried. Throughout the lobby, heads turned. Moments later, four familiar figures emerged from the crowd. The Lexus quartetette was at her side before Yaker knew what was happening.

They let loose with a barrage of questions. "Is this guy bothering you, Liz?" "You want us to take care of him?" "Are you going to get lost right now, Mister, or do we have to persuade you?"

Their commanding stance and the tone of their voices left no doubt they were ready to target Yaker's oversized nose. After casting a venomous glance at Liz, he slunk off without a word and disappeared into the crowd.

"Thanks, guys," Liz said.

"Our pleasure," Wait replied.

"It would have been more of a pleasure to let him have it between the eyes," Larry added. "Who is he, anyway? Did you get his name?"

Liz nodded. "Yaker—he's a reporter with *The National Informer.* Somehow, he got the idea that I'm a New York detective."

All four burst into laughter.

"We know who told him that," Dennis said. "Pedro!"

"Yeah," Jim said. "He told us the same thing."

"Speaking of detectives, this morning Walt and I had a second interview with the sheriff and one of those cop friends of yours from New York," Larry said.

Liz had to think for a moment before recalling that Larry had met Ike and Ralph when he volunteered to help in the search. Then another thought struck her. When Larry was called in for a second interview, he must have known some-one had blabbed to the sheriff about his intense dislike for Buford. Maybe he thought it was one of his friends. She should confess, she decided.

Before she could gather the words, Larry continued. "I've made no secret of my feelings toward Buford. Apparently, I was overheard one of the several times I referred to him as a louse, or worse."

"Pedro again," Dennis said with a grin.

Larry nodded. "Apparently it got back to the sheriff and he wanted to check it out. I admitted I wasn't shedding any tears over Buford and I told him why."

Liz was about to ask him why he disliked Buford, when Walt broke in. "The sheriff also wanted to know how come I didn't tell him, in my first interview, that Larry hates Buford's guts. I told him it didn't occur to me because I didn't believe old Larry was capable of murder. If he was he'd have bumped Buford off more than a year ago."

What had happened a year ago to turn Larry against Buford Doakes?

The question had barely crossed her mind when Larry provided the answer. "My kid sister and a bunch of other teenaged girls went to one of Buford's concerts. My sister's a cute little girl, but very unsophisticated compared to most girls her age. She caught Buford's eye and she was invited to a party in his hotel after the show." He paused. His face clouded. "She was barely eighteen and that SOB got her so drunk she blacked out—didn't know what was happening. He took her to his room . . ."

Liz couldn't express her feelings in words. She just shook her head.

"Fortunately, someone intervened," Larry went on. "Sis

thinks it was Buford's manager. He sobered her up with coffee, got some food into her, then put her in a cab and sent her home. But every time I think about what could have happened, I see red."

Kohner had a decent side to him, Liz thought.

"Liz, we heard you and Sophie got lost while you were hiking yesterday and didn't get back till dinnertime," Jim said. "And Larry helped look for you."

Larry gave a rueful smile. "I wanted to be the big hero and find you."

"Thanks for pitching in," Liz said. "Ike and Ralph appreciated your help, and Sophie too."

"Where's Sophie this morning?" Walt asked.

"She and Ralph are around here somewhere," Liz replied. Wherever they were, she hoped it was someplace where they wouldn't be disturbed.

"Ralph's the man she's engaged to, right?" Dennis asked.

"Right. They're getting married in October."

"And the other cop—where does he fit in?"

Good question, Liz thought. How would Ike have answered it? An awkward silence was averted when Walt looked at his watch, saying they had a ten o'clock tee-off time and they should get moving.

"Thanks for running that obnoxious character off," Liz said.

"You better find Sophie and her fiancé before he shows up again," Larry said, as they turned to leave.

It wasn't likely that Yaker would bother her again, Liz thought, watching the four of them disappear into the throng. After his ignominious departure, he'd probably decided to look for another source of information. He could have gone anywhere on the inn premises, but she guessed that he'd decided that Pedro was his best bet and was waiting for him to finish his dining room duty.

She thought of Larry, again. Would he have waited more than a year to get his revenge on Buford, especially when his sister had emerged relatively unharmed? Also, he hadn't given any indication that he knew why she and Sophie were so late coming back from their hike. Most likely Ike and

Andy had taken all this into consideration and eliminated him as a suspect. She decided she would, too.

One down and seven to go. She hoped today's interviews would lead Ike and Andy to cross some others off the list. Either way, with so many on the list, prospects seemed slim of a prime suspect emerging by three o'clock that afternoon.

She'd been so deep in thought that she hadn't noticed anyone nearby till she heard a voice say, "Hi, Liz." She turned and saw Gail, tennis racket in hand.

"I was hoping I'd run into you," Gail said. "It was all over the inn that you and Sophie lost your way on the trail yesterday and were missing for hours. I was glad to hear you made it back okay."

"Yes, we returned none the worse for the experience," Liz replied. As she spoke, she watched Gail's face for a fleeting expression, a sign that Gail knew what the experience was. She was usually quick on such pickups, but Gail's face showed nothing but friendly concern.

"Another thing going around is that you and Sophie are New York detectives," Gail went on. "And you sent for two more New York detectives to help you and the sheriff find out who drowned Buford." She paused, as if waiting for Liz to confirm this.

Another variation of Pedro's twisted information, Liz thought. She might as well set Gail straight. "That's not exactly true," she replied. "We're all helping, but only one of us is a NYPD detective. The sheriff's an old friend of his and he's doing this as a favor. The other man's a cop but not a detective, and the same goes for Sophie."

Gail's dark eyes gave her a penetrating look. "And what about you?"

"I have absolutely nothing to do with law enforcement. I just like to follow murder cases."

Gail smiled. "Well, that's good. When I heard you were a detective I thought you were the one who set me up for a second interview. I can't believe they thought I might have committed murder. Did you know I was under suspicion?"

"I knew you were on the list," Liz replied. "But so were a bunch of others. How'd your interview go today?"

"Okay, I think. The sheriff told me he'd let me know, later, if I could leave with my friends this afternoon."

That sounded as if Gail had almost been crossed off Andy's list, Liz thought. Good. The idea of this stable, intelligent woman sneaking back to the penthouse and drowning Buford because of a racial slur had seemed improbable to her from the start.

"Well, I'm off to meet my friends on the court," Gail said. "See you later, Liz."

The crowd in the lobby had thinned. Guests who'd been detained by the sheriff had checked out. Recently arrived newspeople had registered and gone to their rooms or into the dining room. She scanned the area for Yaker but he wasn't there. Whatever she decided to do now, he wouldn't see her and follow her around, again.

The morning had developed into a perfect midsummer day. Sunshine sparkled on the lake, and a light breeze rippled its light blue water. Liz considered going out onto the verandah again to enjoy the view and concentrate on the case. Instead, she decided to go for a walk along the lakeshore. She might as well enjoy this beautiful place while she was still here.

She went out through the parking area to the trail she and Sophie had so happily followed back to the inn last evening. Retracing their footsteps over the pine-needled path, she recalled their hours in the cave. How lucky they'd been to get out of there, unharmed. Sophie could have succumbed to her fear of dark, closed-in spaces and become a quivering, hysterical basket case, incapable of the teamwork that got them out. And her own fear of snakes could have made *her* incapable, too.

There was no telling how long they'd have been in there. When the perpetrator locked the icehouse door, he or she didn't know two more NYPD cops were going to show up. If this person was Buford's killer, he or she might have been attempting to avoid what he believed would be a NYPD style investigation led by two slick New York female detectives. Counting on the local sheriff being a bungling hick, maybe he planned to sneak back and release them after the investigation ended and the case left unsolved and cold. Or maybe he counted on two women being so traumatized by their experience that they'd head back to New York as fast as they could. But the appearance of two more NYPD cops, both males, must have put the killer in a quandary.

Locking them in the cave was a stupid move, she thought. Whoever did it had faulty reasoning power.

Even a couple of days and nights in the cave would have taken a heavy toll. The only food they had was one granola bar. Their water bottles were close to empty. They could have become weak and severely dehydrated. And suppose they'd suffered snakebites!

She dismissed thoughts of their plight from her mind and turned her attention to the scenic surroundings. This was truly a place of natural beauty, she thought. She would have liked to climb up to the waterfall, but she wasn't wearing her hiking boots. Besides, there wasn't time to get up there and back before the meeting with Ike and Andy at the crime scene.

She followed the trail through stands of tall pines, glimpsing the lake through the trees, hearing only her own soft footfalls and the call of birds on the wing. Around a bend in the path, she saw a fallen tree and realized she'd come to the place where she and Sophie sat down to rest, just before she noticed the icehouse door.

It was surprising she'd been able to see it, she thought, looking through the dense foliage of the wooded slope. Even now, knowing the cave was there, she could barely make out the outlines of the weathered door. She smiled, recalling how they'd crawled out through the opening they'd made between door and jamb.

She was about to continue her walk when she heard a slight sound as out of place in this quiet spot as rap music on a church organ. It wasn't the whirring of a bird's wings as it flew, startled, from its nest. It wasn't the rustling of leaves in a sudden summer breeze. It wasn't the scurrying of a squirrel or rabbit through the underbrush. It was an unmistakable human cough and it had come from the direction of the old icehouse. Someone was up there at the cave door.

Her instincts screamed at her. *Get away from here on the double.* Who else could be nosing around the old icehouse but Buford's killer, the person who locked you in there? He's probably checking to make sure nothing incriminating had been left at the scene. *You don't want him to see you.*

In the fleeting look she allowed herself before heeding her instincts, she glimpsed a human figure, indistinct because of the foliage, standing near the cave door. Good sense mingled with fear overcame her need to identify it. She jumped up from the log and fled down the trail toward the inn.

Chapter Fourteen

She ran as fast as she'd ever run before, and didn't look back. That would be risky, she thought. What if the person snooping around the icehouse door had seen her? What if he'd recognized her and assumed she'd be able to identify him? If he were now pursuing her, turning around would slow her pace. She might even stumble. The thought of being overtaken by Buford's killer spurred her on. She had to keep on running as fast as she could till she got close enough to the inn to call for help, if necessary.

Those minutes seemed the longest she'd ever known. Only when the trail ended at the road leading to the parking lot, and she saw people within earshot, did she slow down and look over her shoulder. The woodsy trail behind her was deserted.

She hurried across the road into the parking area and sank down on a bench near the inn entrance to catch her breath. Gradually, her heart stopped racing and she started to feel a little foolish. The person she'd glimpsed at the icehouse door might have been one of Andy's deputies. Andy might have sent him there to look for possible fingerprints or footprints. Sure, Andy said they should keep the cave incident strictly among the five of them, but he might not have meant to exclude his men. It made sense he'd want the cave checked out.

At their meeting in the penthouse, she'd ask him if he'd sent one of his men to check out the cave, she decided. If he said yes, she'd keep mum. Otherwise, she'd tell him.

She was about to leave the bench and go inside when she had second thoughts. Maybe she should hang around out here a little longer to see if anyone emerged from the trail. She turned to look across the road and saw two hikers—a middle-aged couple—coming off the trail. Behind them came a trio of young women. She should have started watching sooner, she thought. The killer might have appeared while her back was turned.

He or she couldn't have gone inside without her seeing him. That meant he would still be here in the parking area, perhaps hiding among the parked vehicles or attempting to blend in with the people getting in and out of their cars.

Was her imagination overacting? Maybe whoever she'd seen back there at the icehouse had been unaware of her presence and hadn't pursued her. Or maybe he was a sheriff's deputy.

She rose from the bench and headed for the entrance when a familiar voice sounded from behind her. "Allo. You come back from walk?" She turned to see Pedro, trundling an empty luggage cart toward the entrance.

"Yes, along the lakeshore," she replied. She was surprised he didn't ask if she'd been out running. He must have noticed she looked disheveled.

Instead, he flashed a toothy smile. "You not get lost again, like before when you walk with lady police."

She returned the smile. "No, not this time." His mention of Sophie made her wonder if Sophie and Ralph might be in the lobby. It was getting near the time for their eleven o'clock meeting at the crime scene. "Have you seen my friend around, Pedro?" she asked.

He shook his head. "No. In dining room was last time I see the lady police."

Sophie and Ralph must still be enjoying their time alone, she thought. Pedro kept tabs on everyone's comings and goings. If they were in the lobby, he'd know.

She still felt unnerved and was sure she looked a sweaty mess after running away from the cave and a possible pursuer. A shower and a change of clothes would perk her up. "If you see her, will you tell her I've gone to our room?" she asked.

"Sure, I tell her," Pedro replied. He sprang to open the door for her, before wheeling the cart into the lobby.

By now, Ike and Andy would have background information on the two guards, she thought, as she stepped onto the elevator. If nothing incriminating showed up, they'd be off the suspect list. That would leave Bonnie Lou, Sporn, and Kohner. And Pedro. They always seemed to forget Pedro. She recalled Andy was hoping to find out if he was from Texas and if he might possibly have known Buford before this fateful weekend.

Walking down the corridor to their room, she found herself hoping Andy had, indeed, sent someone to check out the cave. That way she wouldn't have to mention that she'd gone for a walk along the lakeside, alone, and paused on the trail below the cave. Ike would never have to know she'd heard a cough in the woods and glimpsed someone at the cave door, most likely the killer, snooping around. He had a long enough list of dangerous situations she'd gotten herself into. Even though this time, she'd averted the danger, he'd add this to the others and remind her of it every chance he got.

When she entered the room she found Sophie there, flipping TV channels. "Hi. I just got here and I'm trying to find some news coverage on the case," she said. "So far there've only been repeats of the first bulletin. No mention of suspects or anything like that, and the only photos have been old shots of Buford."

"The news about his secret marriage to Bonnie Lou should be breaking soon," Liz replied. "You can bet every reporter here will be dying to get some shots of her, but she's staying holed up in her room."

"Yeah, like everyone else connected to Buford," Sophie said. She turned away from the TV screen and looked at Liz. "What did you do all morning? You look beat."

"I guess I am." Liz described her near encounter with the person snooping around the cave.

Sophie stared at her, wide-eyed. "Wow—that must have been the killer!"

"Unless Andy sent one of his men there. We'll find out when we see him at the crime scene."

"I wish I'd been with you," Sophie said. An instant later, she smiled. "Well, actually, I don't. Ralph and I spent a lovely morning together."

Liz smiled back at her. "That's good. If Ike hadn't been tied up with Andy, maybe I'd have had a lovely morning, too."

Suddenly she thought of the morning's other incident, with Yaker of *The National Informer*. "That's not the only experience I had today," she said. "Remember that obnoxious reporter in the dining room?"

"How could I forget a combination of Jimmy Durante and Cyrano de Bergerac?" Sophie replied. "What happened?"

Liz told her. "Fortunately, I'm the only one whose name he knows," she added.

"But he could write an article about you," Sophie said. "You better tell Andy so he can set that scandal sheet reporter straight."

"I will." The thought of the meeting in the penthouse started Liz peeling off her clothes. "I have to take a shower," she said. She'd put on the yellow shorts and green and yellow shirt Ike liked, she decided.

Half an hour later she and Sophie met Ralph at the penthouse elevator. One of Andy's men, on guard near the barricade, had been instructed to let them on.

They'd boarded the elevator when Liz saw a familiar face a few feet away, in the lobby—Bulbous Nose, with his camera pointed straight at them. Had he managed to get a shot of them? She knew he had it in for her. If he'd taken a picture, he'd use it, and write an accompanying story packed with lies.

Ralph and Sophie saw him, too. Ralph moved to keep the doors open and started to step off when they saw Andy's deputy spring into action. Politely but firmly, he took the camera away from the reporter, removed the film and returned the camera.

"Isn't that a violation of freedom of the press, or something?" Liz asked, as the elevator doors closed.

"Probably," Ralph replied, with a grin.

In the main area of the penthouse, Ike and Andy were seated in armchairs drawn up to a table strewn with coffee mugs, loose papers and a laptop.

Ike rose from his chair when they entered. "Hello, everyone," he said, his eyes focused directly on Liz.

The look in his eyes told her he was glad to see her—and not just because he wanted to get on with the investigation. "Hello," she replied, feeling happy.

"Hi, you two," Sophie said, eyeing the papers on the table. "What's new?"

"Looks like you got the background information from Texas," Ralph added.

"We got full reports on the two guards," MacDuff replied. "Nothing on Pedro, yet." He gestured toward the bar. "Help yourselves to coffee, and then we'll get going on what we found out."

Ike and Andy should be told about the tabloid reporter's attempt to get a photo of them, Liz thought. "Before we start, something happened a few minutes ago that you should know about," she said, as she, Sophie, and Ralph filled mugs from the coffeemaker.

"If it concerns the news photographer who tried to get a shot of you downstairs, Andy's man just phoned and told us," Ike said. "Don't worry, he'll destroy the film."

"Do you have any idea why he wanted a photo of you three?" MacDuff asked.

Liz related her encounter with Yaker. "He's with *The National Informer*. He's convinced that Sophie and Ralph and I are all detectives, moonlighting out of our territory without the knowledge or sanction of our precinct lieutenant or anybody else," she replied. "I believe I'm the only one whose name he knows. Maybe he planned to use the photo to identify Sophie and Ralph."

"I've had run-ins with *Informer* reporters," Ike said. "They'll try anything to get something sensational. Once, one of them almost got through to a crime scene, all set to shoot photos of the corpse before it was even cold."

"You said he *almost* got through. How did you stop him?" MacDuff asked.

Ike gave a satisfied grin. "Let's just say my name is a four-letter word around that rag. It's just as well this reporter doesn't know I'm here."

"We'll try and keep it that way," MacDuff said.

But Yaker was the least of Liz's worries. She still felt shaken by her experience near the cave. "Now, I need to ask you something, Andy," she said. "Did you send one of your men to check out the icehouse, today?"

"Yes, he was there early this morning," MacDuff replied.

"How early?"

"Before seven." He looked at her curiously. "Why?"

"I saw someone there around ten twenty-five."

"It wasn't Charlie. He was on duty at the elevator by seven-thirty."

"Could it have been your other deputy?"

"No. He didn't have orders to check the icehouse, and he's not coming on till noon, anyway."

During this exchange, Liz was aware of Ike staring at her. The expression on his face told her he'd figured out she'd gone to the cave, and added this to the other dangerous situations she'd gotten herself into.

"I didn't actually go near the cave," she told him. "I just went for a walk and when I passed the area where the cave is I stopped and looked up into the woods and then . . ."

"What were you thinking, taking off on the trail, alone, with a killer on the loose?" he asked, his voice a medley of curiosity, exasperation, and concern. "And stopping and hanging around just below the cave? Why in the hell did you do that?"

Ike seldom used profanity when he was with her, much less

direct it at her. His obvious anger didn't upset her. Instead, she felt somewhat pleased. It meant he cared about her.

"Quit badgering her, Ike," Sophie said. "I'd have been right there with her if Ralph hadn't been here."

"It's a damn good thing I *was* here," Ralph said. "The two of you would have been talking and laughing and whoever was snooping around the cave might have heard you and . . ."

"And attacked us? It would have been two against one," Sophie retorted.

"That wouldn't have worked if whoever it was had a gun," Ralph replied.

"If it was Bonnie Lou, I don't believe she'd be packing a gun," Sophie said. "Liz, do you have any idea of the person's size?"

"No," Liz replied. "I could barely make out someone standing at the door and I didn't hang around to get a better look."

MacDuff's voice rose above the discussion. "Liz, this is going to help us. Whoever you saw at the icehouse is most likely the killer. What we need to do now is review the time each of our interviews took place."

He consulted his notes. "Sophie, I know you suspect Bonnie Lou, but we were in her room interviewing her at ten-thirty."

Sophie was not ready to give up on Bonnie Lou. "She could have been in cahoots with someone, and that's who Liz saw."

"Let's go down the list," Ike said. "We interviewed Larry, Walt, and Gail, one by one, in the manager's office, starting with Walt at eight-fifteen. He wasn't a suspect. We wanted to see if his answers lined up with Larry's. We were done with them by eight thirty-five and Gail at ten to nine."

"That's a wide window of opportunity for Gail or Larry," Ralph said.

Liz shook her head. "Neither of them could have been at the icehouse when I got there. Larry was playing golf with his friends at ten o'clock, and I saw Gail in the lobby around ten. We talked for a few minutes and then she went to play tennis."

"Okay," MacDuff said. "We interviewed the guards between nine and twenty after. They're both taking Buford's death hard. They told us they're not going to leave their rooms today."

"Did you get their background reports?" Liz asked.

"Yup. Both men are long time friends of Buford's. They all grew up together in Texas. Been his bodyguards since he first started needing protection from female fans. Ike and I agree there's no reason to suspect either of them. They're both loyal friends, and like I said, they're taking his death hard."

The mention of Texas made Liz think of Pedro's possible connection to Buford. "When do you think you'll get word from Texas about Pedro?" she asked.

"Could be any time now," MacDuff replied.

"Time wise, Pedro could have been at the icehouse when you were there, Liz," Ike said. "But if there's no Texas connection, it's not likely he's the one."

"With no Texas connection to Pedro, that would leave Buford's manager and his music arranger," Sophie said.

Ike looked at his notes again. "Either one of them could have made it to the icehouse before Liz got there. Sporn's interview was over at nine thirty-five. Then we went to Pedro and then Kohner."

"I think we're wasting time on Sporn," Sophie said. "For one thing, he didn't have a key to the penthouse."

"Maybe he used Kohner's key," Liz replied.

MacDuff looked dubious. "They have separate rooms, but I guess it's possible."

Ike gave a slight nod. "Yeah, I suppose he could have sneaked it."

They both sounded as if they, too, thought they might be wasting time on Sporn, Liz thought.

She recalled her encounter with Erwin Sporn on the verandah. Though she hadn't noticed the exact time, Ike's notes indicated Sporn could have made it to the icehouse after he hurried off. She remembered thinking his face had flushed red from embarrassment when he realized his intimate conversation had been overheard. Now she thought the flush might have come from the shock of seeing her. Knowledge of the cave experience was restricted. Their safe return was also being kept quiet. Even though Pedro knew about it and was spreading the word, maybe the word hadn't reached the person who'd locked them in the cave. Was the music arranger that person? Did the sight of one of the women he believed was still locked in the cave send him rushing there in startled bewilderment?

She should run the encounter and these ideas past the others, she thought. But, after thinking things over, she decided they didn't add up. Sporn's arrangements of Buford's vocal performances, especially Buford's own hit song, "True Blue Texas Love," had made him wealthy. Having hitched his wagon to a star, he'd want that star to shine for a long, long time and write more hit songs for him to arrange. And she mustn't forget he didn't have a key to the penthouse.

On the other hand, Kohner did. Was it possible Buford and his manager had a falling out? Was Buford planning to fire Kohner? Maybe Kohner had taken out a life insurance policy on his valuable client. If he had, Andy's Private Eye would find out about it.

"So where do we stand, now?" Ralph asked.

"Larry, Bonnie Lou, and the guards are off the list, and we're considering scratching Gail," MacDuff replied. "Background reports on Kohner, Sporn, and Pedro should be coming in on the computer, soon."

"What if some of the information is too hush-hush to send over the Internet?" Liz asked.

"Andy's P.I. uses initials instead of names in his reports," Ike replied.

"I still think Bonnie Lou figures in here, somewhere," Sophie insisted. "I realize she couldn't have been at the cave if she was being interviewed at ten-thirty, but like I said before, maybe she was in cahoots with somebody—one of the guards, maybe. I know they've been checked out and they're off the list, but . . ."

"The person Liz saw couldn't have been a guard. Both of them said they were going to stay in their rooms today," Ralph reminded her.

"Sure, that's what they said," Sophie retorted. "But one of them could have sneaked out."

"Looks like we can't go any further till those background reports come in," MacDuff said. "What do you say we call room service and order lunch?"

"Good idea, I'm starved," Sophie replied.

Ike got to his feet, saying "I saw some menus over on the bar by the phone."

Pedro wouldn't miss a chance of horning in on the meeting he undoubtedly knew was in progress, Liz thought. He'd manage to be the one who delivered their lunch. She hoped he didn't wheel in the cart just as his background report came onto the computer screen. What was holding up that report? she wondered. Information on the guards had been received from Texas some time ago.

She and Sophie ordered club sandwiches and iced tea. The men opted for Reubens and beers. While they waited for the delivery, Liz and Sophie agreed they'd like to look around the penthouse. Neither of them had seen the area beyond the main room and the hot tub area.

"Andy, is it okay if we go into the bedrooms and bathrooms?" Liz asked.

"Sure, we're done back there," MacDuff replied. "But don't disturb anything. I want everything left as is for awhile, in case I want to double check them again."

While Liz and Sophie headed for the bedrooms, Sophie remarked that Andy might not have totally given up on Bonnie Lou as the killer. "Why else would he be thinking of double checking her bedroom?" she asked.

There was no budging Sophie away from her idea that petite Bonnie Lou had somehow managed to drown Buford, Liz thought. But at least Sophie had latched firmly onto a suspect, unlike the others, who, like herself, seemed to be in a quandary.

She looked at her watch. Only three hours and twenty minutes before checkout time. They'd all be disappointed, especially Ike, if they couldn't pin down a prime suspect before they left.

She and Sophie looked around the bedrooms and baths. They'd been left as they were when Bonnie Lou and the guards moved to other rooms. No housekeeping personnel had been allowed into the penthouse yet.

In the guards' room, drapes were still drawn over the windows and beds were a shambles of spreads, sheets, blankets and pillows. Cigarette butts littered ashtrays. A miasma of stale tobacco smoke hung in the air. In their bathroom, soggy towels drooped askew on racks and slimy soap wallowed on the sink.

In Buford's quarters, sunlight streamed through open draperies and it appeared as if Bonnie Lou had attempted to make the king-size bed and straighten up their bathroom before she left.

Liz cast a teasing look at Sophie. "She may be a killer but she's tidy."

"She was probably destroying evidence," Sophie snapped back.

They were on their way back to the main room when Liz heard a voice in the foyer calling "room service!" No familiar "allo." *Not Pedro's voice.*

"I'm surprised Pedro passed up the chance to bring lunch to the crime scene," she said to Sophie.

At that moment they saw Ralph standing near the hot tub. Sophie joined him and Liz started walking over to sit with Ike. She noticed he was engrossed in his notes—too engrossed to pay any attention to the man in the room service jacket, who wheeled the lunch cart into the room.

MacDuff greeted the man. "Right over here will be fine," he said, indicating a spot near the seating area. Though he was face-to-face with the room service waiter, he showed no reaction. He'd never seen this man before.

But Liz had. She gasped and stared in disbelief. The man was Bulbous Nose.

Chapter Fifteen

Liz knew he hadn't noticed her. His eyes were fixated on Ike, and Ike, still absorbed in his notes, hadn't looked up. Liz thought the scandal sheet reporter seemed startled for a moment before his beady eyes narrowed and a malevolent look crossed his face.

The look told her that Yaker of *The National Informer* recognized Eichle of the NYPD. He had to be the reporter Ike had ejected from a homicide scene.

What happened next took only seconds. As Yaker removed a dish from the cart, and flourished a napkin, Liz was struck with a realization. There was a camera under that napkin! She lunged at him and knocked the dish from his hand.

Dish and napkin fell to the floor, drawing Ike's attention away from his notes. He and MacDuff looked at her in puzzlement. She heard Ike's voice. "Liz, what the . . . ?"

He stopped short when the presumed waiter hastily picked up the fallen dish and napkin and hurriedly headed for the foyer. In those few moments Ike must have gotten a good look at him, Liz thought, and he'd probably seen the camera, too.

"That's no waiter, that's a reporter from the *Informer*. The SOB was going to shoot my picture!" Ike bellowed, leaping to his feet and taking off in pursuit.

MacDuff followed. Sophie and Ralph had rushed over

from the hot tub when they heard Ike yell. They appeared just in time to realize the fleeing man was the obnoxious reporter they'd encountered at breakfast. When sounds of a scuffle came from the foyer, Ralph took off to join the fray.

"Well, at least the big schnoz brought our lunch," Sophie said, eyeing the food cart. "How did he get past Andy's deputy and why did he want Ike's picture?"

"Andy called down and told his deputy we were expecting room service," Liz replied. "The reporter must have bribed Pedro and borrowed his jacket. He knew the four supposed detectives were meeting up here—he saw three of us on the elevator."

It was surprising that Pedro would pass up another chance to find out what was happening in the penthouse, she thought. Yaker must have paid him plenty.

"I get it," Sophie said. "He's one of the reporters Ike told us he tangled with. He didn't know Ike was with us. When he saw Ike, he decided to get a shot of him, first."

Liz nodded. "But he intended to get all four of us very quickly and leave before anyone recognized him."

"Yeah, who really looks at the room service guy?" Sophie asked. "But lucky you did, or he could have taken our pictures and split without anyone knowing he had a hidden camera."

"He doesn't have anyone's name but mine, and I guess he wanted to identify the other three," Liz said. "He thought if he could get shots of you, he could find out your names through the Department. He was planning to write an exposé on corruption in the NYPD." She gave a wry smile. "What would he have done when he found out that Ike's the only detective and I'm not even on the force?"

"That wouldn't matter to him or his sleazy tabloid," Sophie replied. "He would have gone ahead and run the story anyway, pictures and all."

Ralph's voice sounded from the doorway. "No chance of that now. Andy phoned his deputy and he's on his way up to escort our bogus waiter down to the lobby and make sure the manager asks him to check out."

"I hope you accidentally smashed his camera," Sophie said.

"Sorry—not that we didn't want to. We took all his film, though. He had a couple of new rolls in his pocket besides what was in the camera."

A worrisome thought plagued Liz. No doubt Yaker knew the identity of the NYPD detective who'd forcibly removed him from a crime scene. He wanted to get even. In the penthouse, he'd recognized Ike. He wouldn't need a picture to write a scurrilous article about a top NYPD detective working on a murder case outside New York. He'd make it sound as if Ike had done this secretly for big bucks, pretending he was taking emergency time off.

Ike and MacDuff appeared at that moment. "Well, let's have our lunch," Ike said. He and Ralph took the coffee mugs off the table and cleared away some of the papers to make room.

As they seated themselves around the table with their sandwiches and beverages, Ike looked at Liz with a big smile and took her hand. "Nice work," he said.

His touch and his smile warmed her heart. "Thanks, but I have a feeling this isn't over," she replied. "I figured that tabloid reporter's the one you threw out of the crime scene."

He gave her hand a gentle squeeze. "You're right, but don't worry—it will be over after I contact the station house and run it by the lieutenant. I know he'll say there's nothing wrong with helping a friend look into a case on off time."

"Except for him, the media reporters have been okay," MacDuff said. "They've been very patient. The only news they have is Buford's secret marriage. I let them in on that this morning. It should be on radio and TV by now."

"We thought Yaker had a scoop on the marriage," Sophie said. She related what happened in the dining room at breakfast.

MacDuff shook his head. "I met with reporters this morning, before we started our interviews. Apparently Yaker wasn't there, or he'd have known about the marriage."

"Evidently he got tired of waiting for a legitimate story and decided to nose around for something on his own," Liz replied. She laughed. "Then, when Pedro mentioned Buford's secret marriage, he really believed he had a big scoop."

MacDuff nodded, with a wry grin. "Yup, while he's thinking about his big scoop, Buford's marriage will hit the headlines and networks way ahead of it."

"I'd love to see his face when he finds out he was scooped on his scoop," Sophie said.

"Not me, I never want to see that big schnozzola again!" Liz exclaimed.

"Most reporters aren't like him," MacDuff said. "Most of them are okay. Later on this afternoon I'm going to let them know how things stand."

It was unlikely he'd be able to announce an arrest in the case, Liz thought. Again she wished they could come up with a strong suspect before they left Lorenzo's. But time was running out. What could possibly develop in three hours to nail down one of the three remaining suspects as the killer?

Sophie finished her sandwich and got out of her chair. "Let's watch TV and see how the case is being covered," she said, turning on a nearby television set.

Buford's secret marriage was in full play. Old photos of Bonnie Lou had been dredged up from the Gulch City High School annual. Shots of Buford and Bonnie Lou at their Senior Prom were shown, as well as photos of a teenaged Buford playing his guitar in one of the local bars.

Bonnie Lou's parents were interviewed. Her mother said news of the marriage didn't surprise her. They'd been dating since junior high and she knew they'd get married some day. When asked why she thought the marriage had been kept secret, she said she was sure Buford wanted it that way.

"I don't mean to speak ill of the dead, but Buford was a mighty good-looking boy and he knew it. Girls always made a big fuss over him, and he liked it. Even though he stuck with Bonnie Lou all these years, he wanted his teenaged girl fans to believe he was single," she said.

Bonnie Lou's father expressed disappointment that Bonnie Lou and Buford weren't married in the Gulch City Community church they'd attended since childhood. He disagreed with his wife about whose idea the secret marriage was.

"Buford wouldn't have kept the marriage a secret without pressure from that manager of his," he added. He said there was no doubt in his mind that Sid Kohner had insisted on the secrecy. He'd wondered for some time when Buford was going tell Kohner to stop running his life. Lately, he'd been hopeful about that. In a recent phone call from Bonnie Lou she'd told them Buford was getting fed up with his manager and was thinking of making a change.

Aha! Liz's senses went on alert. Her idea that Buford and Kohner might have had a falling out wasn't so farfetched after all!

Interviews with members of Buford's family came on. His parents were on their way to Pennsylvania to assist Bonnie Lou with arrangements for transporting the body back to Texas, but Buford's brother, and numerous aunts, uncles, and cousins, spoke freely about Gulch City's boy who'd made it big in showbiz.

Buford's relatives provided further evidence that all was not peaches and cream between Buford and Kohner. They all said Buford had remarked, recently, that his brother could do a better job than Sid Kohner.

Liz felt sure she was on to something. And what if Kohner's background report showed that he'd taken out an insurance policy on Buford's life?

While these thoughts whirled around in her head, Ike was still holding her hand. Now he released it with a gentle pat and looked into her eyes. "You've been very quiet the last few minutes. Something tells me you've come up with an idea," he said.

Surely, she wasn't the only one who'd picked up on the possibility of a rift between Buford and Kohner, she thought. They'd all heard the newscast. She looked around the table. "I guess you're all thinking maybe Buford was ready to fire Kohner and Kohner knew it," she said.

MacDuff nodded his head. "Yup, Ike and I were talking about that before you got here. One of the guards told us Buford and Kohner had been arguing. Kohner insisted that Buford cut out partying with teenaged groupies after his concerts. Evidently there'd been some trouble that had to be hushed up."

"Kohner told Buford if he had to throw parties on tour they must be held the night before the concert, with no teenagers invited—just young women," Ike added. "That's when Buford threatened to give him the boot."

"And the relatives' statements on TV back it up," MacDuff said.

Ralph gave a low whistle. "Sounds like we have a dark horse suspect."

Sophie was the lone dissenter. "Bonnie Lou had more motive and opportunity than Kohner."

"Maybe you'll change your mind after we get the report on him," Ike said.

"Let's sum up what we have on Kohner so far," MacDuff suggested. "First, there's the possibility that he knew he was going to be fired."

"Second, he had a key to the penthouse," Ike added.

"And he's a fairly big man," Liz said. "His arms are long enough to reach into the tub and grab Buford's ankles." She glanced at Sophie as she spoke. Sophie was stubborn as a mule about Bonnie Lou, she thought. Motive and opportunity notwithstanding, she wouldn't admit that Buford's secret bride was too small and frail to have done the drowning.

Sophie glanced toward the plants surrounding the hot tub. "I can't picture any man bothering to pick up that overturned pot, least of all Kohner," she said. "He's too much of a slob to do that."

Liz had to agree. Kohner always looked rumpled, as if he'd slept in his clothing and he kept his pockets stuffed with heaven knows what. She recalled how he'd approached them in the lobby, digging into one of those bulging pockets for his business cards and inadvertently spilling out a half-empty pack of cigarettes and some wadded-up chewing gum wrappers. He'd picked up the pack of smokes but left the gum wrappers on the floor.

But she wasn't ready to dismiss Kohner yet. She'd wait to see if he'd taken out a policy on Buford's life. Since this was a Sunday, would the background reports they were waiting for include such information? "Andy, will your P.I. have access to business transactions on a Sunday?" she asked.

MacDuff nodded. "With his sources and connections, he can get anything he's after, any day of the week."

"Just what sort of business transaction did you have in mind, Liz?" Ike asked. His grin told her he and Andy had thought of the life insurance policy, and he suspected she had, too.

"I'm sure you already know I think Kohner might have insurance on Buford's life," she replied.

"Life insurance!" Sophie exclaimed. "Why didn't I think of that?"

"You were too much into Bonnie Lou," Liz replied.

"Well, I still am," Sophie retorted. "Buford probably had a huge life insurance policy with Bonnie Lou the beneficiary."

There was no prying Sophie away from her favorite suspect, Liz thought. But she had a point here. If Bonnie Lou knew she was a beneficiary, she'd have an additional motive for murder. A few more inches on her petite stature and twenty more pounds on her frame, and Sophie's insistence might make some sense.

"We already know Buford had life insurance, and Bonnie Lou is the sole beneficiary," MacDuff said. "But the policy isn't very big."

"And neither is the rest of his estate," Ike added. "According to Kohner, Buford had a modest bank account and a few investments. Certainly not enough to kill for."

"But he was making millions," Sophie said.

"Yup, and spending it as fast as it came in," MacDuff replied. "Drugs and booze don't come cheap."

Sophie was silent for a moment before replying. "Well, even without the money angle, Bonnie Lou had a strong motive. The only way she'd be acknowledged as Buford's wife was to kill him."

"Sophie, sweetheart, you have to accept the fact that she's off the list," Ralph said.

"Not my list," Sophie replied. "Bonnie Lou's at the top and Gail's second. Kohner and Sporn are still on it, but not Pedro."

Gail. Liz had almost forgotten that Ike and Andy considered taking her off the official list. "Have you decided what to do about Gail?" she asked.

"We're waiting till after we get the reports on Pedro, Sporn, and Kohner," MacDuff replied. "If there's incriminating evidence against one of them, we'll cross Gail off."

Liz detected a slight frown on his generally affable face. He must be concerned about the reports, she thought. Would they arrive in time for analyses? Would the information provide what was needed to pin down a prime suspect, maybe even make an arrest before they had to leave?

A sudden thought encouraged her. If the reports weren't complete by checkout time, they could hang around with Andy awhile and continue working on the case. But they had to get on the road that evening. Ike and Ralph were due back on duty early the next morning.

At that moment MacDuff's voice penetrated her thoughts. "Something's coming over the Internet."

Chapter Sixteen

Liz felt her spirits rising. They all crowded around to watch—even Sophie, whose firm belief in Bonnie Lou's guilt evidently didn't affect her curiosity. Would the incoming report contain incriminating evidence on Kohner, or would it shine the spotlight of guilt on Sporn or Pedro?

Initials came up on the screen: S. J. K.

Kohner. Liz took a quick breath.

Ike must have noticed. "Don't get too excited," he said. "The P.I. might not have found anything incriminating."

"Yup," Andy replied. "It could be just a rundown on Kohner to stack up with what we have."

"On the other hand, there could be something in this report that seems innocent on the surface . . ." Ike began.

"But when it's put together with something we already have, it might add up to a clue?" Liz asked.

"Exactly. So let's study each report carefully."

"Looks like Kohner had some lean years before he discovered Buford," Ralph said, as the report unfolded. "He went from New York to Nashville, trying to latch onto some hot talent."

"And he was divorced after only three years and never remarried," Sophie commented. "That doesn't surprise me. What woman would put up with a slob like him?"

Liz knew Sophie was reminding her that it was probably

the killer who'd picked up the fallen plant, and Kohner wouldn't have done this.

The report continued with general information—how Kohner discovered Buford singing in a Gulch City bar and how Buford's overnight success had made them both wealthy. It mentioned that Kohner had moved his promotional activity to Manhattan soon after Buford's first successful recording.

His decision to accompany Buford on tour was also mentioned, along with the likelihood that Kohner wanted to oversee Buford's activities on the road. Then it stated that Kohner had a five-year contract with Buford to manage his career. It touched on rumors of possible discord between the two of them and an attempt by Buford to break the contract. But no mention of an insurance policy on Buford's life.

"So, is Buford's attempt to break the contract enough to keep Kohner on the list?" Liz asked.

"Yeah, I think we should keep him on till we've seen all the reports," Ike replied. "What do you think, Andy?"

"Yup. We shouldn't cross him off yet."

At that moment, their attention was drawn to the TV, which had been left on after the interviews with Buford's family. Since then there'd been nothing but one rehash after another. Now a bulletin came on, announcing that Pennsylvania's governor was greatly distressed over the murder of Buford Doakes, and dissatisfied with the lack of progress in the case. He blamed both the County Sheriff and District Attorney for dragging their feet.

"For Pete's sake, it only happened yesterday!" Liz exclaimed.

"Andy, he hasn't given you half a chance," Ralph added.

"I can understand why he's doing this," MacDuff said. "A celebrity was murdered in his state. Thousands of Pennsylvania residents are fans of Buford's. He has to let them know he feels as shocked and saddened as they do."

At that moment the governor came on with a brief statement. He promised he'd waste no time getting to the bottom of this heinous crime. He would call upon the best detectives in the state to take over. The killer of one of the nation's most talented young stars would be caught and brought to justice, without delay.

This could only mean trouble for Andy, Liz thought. The governor intended to kick him off the case and send in his own investigators. How unfair! Andy's investigation had been in effect considerably less than forty-eight hours.

"The governor's not going to send his troops over here today," MacDuff said, with a wry grin. "We still have time to wrap this up."

Liz felt her spirits sag. What if they didn't wrap it up? Andy would have to turn over all their evidence to the governor's men who'd use it to solve the case in another day or so. The governor's team would get all the credit. The governor would emerge as the big hero who'd stepped in to kick the bungling rural sheriff off the case and make sure the killer of a national celebrity was nabbed without further delay.

Into these discouraging thoughts came sounds from the computer, followed by Andy's voice. "Here's another report!"

The initials E. S. appeared on the screen. The report on Sporn began by saying he was a native of Brooklyn, New York. Present address, Manhattan. Married at age fifty-one to a younger woman. No children.

"Fifty-one," Sophie said. "He doesn't look any older than that, now. He must have been married recently."

And he's crazy about his wife, Liz thought, remembering the one-way phone conversation she'd overheard. She also recalled deciding he was henpecked.

The report went on to say neighbors in the Manhattan apartment complex where Sporn and his wife lived described him as a quiet man, devoted to his wife. One neighbor said Mrs. Sporn was angry because Buford did not allow members of his entourage to bring spouses along on the road, although he always brought his girlfriend. As Buford's music arranger, wouldn't Sporn have been exempt from stipulations applying to musicians and others? Liz wondered. He was so crazy about his wife, why hadn't he insisted on it? Maybe Buford was temperamental. Maybe, to keep him amiable and ensure good performances, they all felt they had to toe the line.

The report continued, saying that for several years Sporn made a fair living assisting with musical arrangements for vocal groups and individual singers. Two years ago he met Sidney Kohner, Buford Doakes' manager, who offered him a job arranging all of Buford's music. That's when he came into his own as a top arranger.

When the report ended, Liz felt surprised that none of the neighbors mentioned his grumpiness. Well, maybe he wasn't grumpy when he was home with his wife, she thought, turning away from the computer and seating herself on the sofa.

The report contained nothing that could have aroused suspicion against Sporn. But she hadn't forgotten that when he rushed off the verandah, he could have gone straight to the cave. "Sporn doesn't seem to have a motive, but I think he should stay on the list," she said.

"He's staying on," MacDuff replied.

"So you still have the same three suspects," Sophie said. "Kohner, Sporn, and Pedro."

She was still disgruntled that Bonnie Lou wasn't on the list, Liz thought.

"While we're waiting for information on Pedro let's go over Gail," Ike said.

"Gail!" Sophie echoed. "I thought you said you and Andy got a thorough check on her yesterday and you were ready to strike her off the list."

Ike glanced at MacDuff. "That's right, but we've been talking it over."

"There's a possibility she could have been the person Liz saw at the cave," MacDuff said.

Liz shook her head. "I saw her leave to play tennis at ten o'clock."

"Did you actually see her on the tennis court?" MacDuff asked.

"Well . . . no . . ."

"We need witnesses," Ike said. "While we're waiting for the report on Pedro, Andy said he'd phone the tennis pro shop and find out what time Gail and her friends were on the court this morning."

"Do they keep a record?" Liz asked.

"Yup," MacDuff replied. "Players reserve the courts for certain times. If Gail was playing at ten, she'd have signed in, along with her friends."

"But we're not depending on that, alone," Ike added, "We have to make sure she played the entire time—that she didn't leave for awhile. If she did, someone would have noticed."

"Chances are she'll check out okay and we can take her off the list," MacDuff said. "We just have to cover all bases."

Liz nodded. "Of course you do. Too bad the governor doesn't know what a thorough job you're doing."

"We still have a few hours to prove it to him," MacDuff said, picking up the phone.

While MacDuff made his call to the tennis pro shop, Ike sat down on the sofa next to Liz. "We haven't had much time together, have we?" he asked. "I mean, other than discussing the case."

What an understatement, she thought. Recalling Pop's wise words, she gave him a smile. "We've both been absorbed in the case—especially you."

He returned the smile. "You're very understanding, Liz. I always thought you were, but now I'm sure of it." He leaned over and gave her a gentle kiss. "We'll have a good talk on the drive back," he said. "Ralph and I figured he and Sophie could take your grandmother's car back to Staten Island and you and I will head for Manhattan in my car. Is that okay with you?"

"Sure," she replied. A couple of hours of uninterrupted time with him sounded much more than okay, even if all they could do was talk.

"I'm still hoping we'll be congratulating each other all the way for helping Andy solve the case," he said.

"I haven't given up hope, either," she replied. "But I'm disappointed I couldn't come up with a nice big clue for you."

"You did. You saw someone nosing around the cave. If we can find out who it was, we'll have our killer."

MacDuff's voice sounded from the direction of the phone. "Well, it wasn't Gail. She and her friends were on the tennis court from ten till eleven."

"I was sure it wasn't Gail," Sophie said.

"So we're back to the same three," Liz said. She couldn't help feeling discouraged. Reports on Kohner and Sporn had given them next to nothing. What if they found the information on Pedro just as lacking? She felt torn between wanting Pedro to be innocent and wanting his report to contain something incriminating.

A sudden flash of memory hit her. After her flight down the trail, away from the cave, while she was sitting on the bench near the entrance, she'd seen Pedro wheeling a luggage cart across the parking area. Had he been the person she'd glimpsed at the old icehouse? Had he seen her and believed she'd identified him, and tried to catch up with her on the trail? Would he have dragged her off the trail, into the woods, and . . . ? The dreadful possibility made her shudder. When she reached the safety of the parking area, had he slipped in among the parked cars while her back was turned?

Ike's voice came into her imaginings. "You look upset all of a sudden. What's the matter?"

She'd never taken seriously the idea of Pedro being the killer. Now, the notion that the genial bellman might be guilty had, indeed, upset her. Reluctantly, she told Ike and Andy her suspicions.

"How did he seem when you saw him with the luggage cart?" MacDuff asked.

"He was pleasant and friendly, like he always is. I guess that's why I didn't think of this at the time."

"Then you didn't give him any reason to believe you saw him at the cave?" Ike asked.

"No. I remember he asked me if I'd been for a walk and I said yes, and he joked about me not getting lost again. Then I asked him if he'd seen Sophie around and when he said he hadn't seen her since breakfast, I said if he saw her would he please tell her I've gone to our room."

"Good," Ike said. "If he's our man, he believes you're no threat to him, but more important, he's no threat to you."

Liz gave a sigh. "This has to be a coincidence. Pedro just happened to be loading luggage into a car when I got there. He's always so friendly and nice."

"So was Ted Bundy," Ike replied.

A sound from the computer drew their attention. "We're getting another report," MacDuff announced.

He didn't have to add that this one was on Pedro.

Chapter Seventeen

W hen the initials "P. R." appeared on the screen, Liz realized she didn't know Pedro's last name. She was about to
ask Andy what it was, when he came up with the answer.

"My investigator had quite a time tracking down the right
Pedro Romero," he said. "There are quite a few men in
Texas by that name."

"Andy got copies of his Personnel records from the hotel
manager for the P.I.," Ike said. "That's how he was able to
trace the right Pedro Romero."

MacDuff studied the screen. "Family came into the U.S.
from Mexico as legal immigrants when Pedro was fourteen,
and settled in El Paso."

"Five children, Pedro the oldest," Ike said. "Father spoke
a few words of English, others only Spanish. I guess the kids
picked up English in school here."

Liz watched the rest of the information come in. Pedro's
father was a farm laborer, mother a domestic. Hard-working,
respectable people. But then she read that Pedro had been in
trouble with the law when he was fifteen. He'd dropped out
of school, the report stated, and gotten in with a rough crowd
of juveniles who were suspected of vandalism and stealing
hubcaps, but there hadn't been enough probable cause for
arresting any of them. When he was seventeen he worked as
a handyman in a jewelry store for a few months, until a piece

of jewelry was reported missing and he was suspected of stealing it. His arrest was imminent when the jewelry was found on the floor under a display case. Pedro was cleared but fired from the job.

"Well at least this isn't as boring as Sporn's report," Sophie said.

Just as she spoke, a startling bit of information rolled down the screen. When he was eighteen, Pedro was with a gang of kids outside a pool parlor when a fight broke out and one of the kids was beaten and stabbed to death. Several reliable adult witnesses at the scene told police that Pedro had nothing to do with it. They'd seen him walking away from the fight before the stabbing occurred.

"So he lucked out, again," Ralph said.

"Look what it says next," Ike replied. "This was a wake-up call for him."

When Liz read the remainder of the report, she had to agree. After this close call, Pedro did a complete turnaround. Because of his bad reputation in El Paso he left there and went east. He found a steady job as bellman in an Atlantic City hotel, stayed out of trouble, worked hard, and regularly sent most of his pay to his family.

"That sounds more like the Pedro we know," Ralph said,

"Yeah, but do we really know him?" Sophie asked. "How come he's up here in the Poconos? Did something happen in Atlantic City? Was he fired from his job?"

This sounded as if Sophie might actually be considering a suspect other than Bonnie Lou, Liz thought.

"If something happened in Atlantic City to get him fired, it would be in the report," MacDuff replied. "This P.I. doesn't miss anything."

Liz continued reading the report. Pedro wanted to work in a rural area. He came to Lorenzo's three years ago. No complaints about him—only praise. Known as an honest, diligent, cheerful worker. She shook her head. "I don't know what to think."

MacDuff perused the report. "And there's no connection between Pedro and either of the guards," he said. "Pedro

never lived anywhere near Gulch City. Buford never appeared in the Atlantic City hotel where Pedro worked. It's
certain they never laid eyes on each other till the day Buford
arrived here."

"There goes the Texas connection," Ralph said.

"And there goes the motive," Liz added.

MacDuff's cell phone rang. "It's the police lab," he said,
checking the caller ID. "They've been trying to lift fingerprints off Buford's hat. Probably calling to tell me what I
was pretty sure of—they couldn't do it."

"Too bad, but you had to give it a try," Ike replied.

It *was* too bad, Liz thought. Most likely only Buford himself had handled his Stetson on that fateful night. But there
was a chance that during the struggle the killer might have
grabbed the hat or touched it. Any prints on it other than Buford's would belong to the person who fought with him and
then drowned him.

MacDuff hung up the phone with a big smile. "Well, what
do you know, they got some prints off the hat that aren't Buford's," he announced.

Liz felt a rush of excitement. Sophie looked interested.
Ike and Ralph looked skeptical.

"Now they can work on getting a match," MacDuff continued. "The night of the drowning we collected drinking glasses
from the penthouse bedrooms and later from the rooms of the
suspects. They were bagged and labeled and sent to the lab."

"How about Pedro's prints?" Liz asked.

MacDuff nodded. "Yup. Got them, too. When I arrived
here the night of the murder, I noticed a room service cart
and saw some serving dishes with aluminum covers. I had
two of them bagged and sent to the lab with the other stuff.
Later, I was told Pedro had been up here delivering food. His
prints should be all over those aluminum covers." He paused
with a broadening smile. "If the prints on the hat match, this
could be the break we've been waiting for."

Liz saw Ike and Ralph exchange doubtful glances. It was
obvious they didn't go along with Andy's enthusiasm. They
were certain that fabric would not hold fingerprints.

MacDuff must have picked up on the glances. He laughed. "I don't blame you for thinking I'm way off base here. I got so excited I forgot to mention the prints were lifted from the *hatband.*"

Ike broke into a grin. "Leather!" he exclaimed.

"Yup—genuine hide, with plenty of space between the diamonds. The lab technician told me the prints are beauties."

"Sounds like someone was trying to get the diamonds," Ralph said. "Remember we touched on the idea that robbery might have been the motive and it went sour when the perp found out the diamonds are fakes."

"But how did the killer find out they aren't real?" Liz asked. "Do you suppose Buford told him?" She pictured Buford taunting the would-be diamond thief.

"Possibly," MacDuff said. "Or maybe the killer knew something about diamonds, and when he got a close look at the stones in the hatband he knew they were fakes."

"But why would he drown Buford just because the diamonds weren't real?" Liz asked. "Did he do it because Buford could identify him to the police?"

Sophie nodded. "Or maybe he flew into a violent rage of frustration."

She was really considering someone other than Bonnie Lou, Liz thought.

MacDuff reviewed the report. He gave a grunt. "Pedro worked in a jewelry store for awhile . . ."

"And he was suspected of stealing a piece of jewelry," Ralph said. "What if he *did* steal it and when he realized the heat was on, hid it under the display case?"

"Suppose he did, and it was diamond jewelry—could he have studied the diamonds and be able to tell the difference between real and fake?" Sophie asked.

"Naaah," Ike replied. "Even some experts have to use a jeweler's device to tell the difference."

"Maybe he stole one of those devices, too," Liz said.

Ike cast her an approving grin. "Your pop would be proud of you," he said.

Her heart warmed. It was almost like he'd said *he* was

proud of her and he liked her input, no matter how far-fetched it might be.

"The police must have been pretty sure Pedro was innocent, or they'd have arrested him," she said.

Sophie laughed. "Pedro might be a killer but he draws the line at stealing."

"How long will it take for the lab to match up the prints?" Liz asked.

"Can't say for sure," MacDuff replied. "It's Sunday. The lab's not on full staff."

At that moment Sophie's cell phone rang. She got it out of her purse and looked at the caller ID. "It's my mother and dad," she said. "I should have called them. They know I'm up here and they've heard about the murder. They're probably imagining the killer striking again and this time I'm the victim."

Liz hadn't called Pop and Mom, either. They'd surely heard about the murder but they were in Florida and they didn't know she was at the scene of the crime.

Apparently Sophie was being scolded over the phone. "I'm sorry, Ma," she said. "I should have let you know I'm okay. Liz is fine, too. There was nothing for you to worry about."

As she spoke, she and Liz looked at each other with a single thought. *Nothing to worry about except the possibility of the killer locking them in a cave.*

A sudden thought struck Liz. She should have phoned Gram. Hardly had this crossed her mind when Sophie handed her the phone. "Here," she said. "Your grandmother wants to talk to you."

Liz knew what had happened. Gram lived near Sophie's parents on Staten Island. The three of them had gotten together for a worry fest.

"Hi Gram," she said. "How are you doing?"

Gram's voice sounded slightly chilled. "I might ask you the same question. I heard about the hot tub murder. I've been worried sick. Why didn't you phone me? I tried to call you but I couldn't get through."

"Oh Gram, I'm sorry. It was very thoughtless of me. But there was no reason for you to worry about me."

"*No reason!* With a homicidal fiend rampaging through the hotel drowning people in their hot tubs? And I know you too well, Liz Rooney. I know you can't resist getting involved in murder cases. Don't try to tell me you aren't into this one, even though you must know you're putting yourself in danger."

She thought of a way to calm Gram down. "I'm in no danger, Gram, Ike's here."

The statement had the desired effect. "Oh, God bless him! Did he drive up there when he heard about the murder?"

"Soon afterwards. Ralph's here too. They came together."

Gram really went for the idea of two NYPD Galahads rushing to save their ladies from danger. "Oh, that's lovely. You and Sophie are lucky to have men like them," she said.

Liz didn't remind her that only Sophie actually "had" one of the noble duo. But that hadn't kept Ike from coming all the way up here, anyway, she thought, with a sudden spurt of optimism.

After she and Gram said goodbye, Ike gave her a curious look. "Did I hear you say you were in no danger because I'm here?"

"Yes, I said that."

"Did you mean it, or were you just placating your grandmother?"

"A little of each, I guess," she replied. "I had to calm Gram down, but I *do* feel safe when you're around."

"I'd like you to feel safe all the time," he said.

Her heart went into a spin. Only the sound of MacDuff's voice halted its whirling. "I've made copies of all the reports. Let's go over Kohner and Sporn while we're waiting for the prints to be matched."

With the fingerprints on the Stetson creating an atmosphere of suspenseful excitement, and on top of that, Ike's somewhat romantic statement, Liz found herself disinterested in going back to the bland reports on Kohner and Sporn. But she took her copies without comment.

"We have to nail down some reasons why each of our suspects would commit this murder," MacDuff said. "We'll begin with Kohner. Why would he want Buford dead?"

The idea that Kohner would kill Buford because of a possible contract termination suddenly seemed illogical to Liz. And without an insurance policy on Buford's life, there was nothing else.

"Kohner wouldn't gain anything by killing Buford," she said. "And it was a five-year contract, wasn't it?"

"Right," Ike said. "Kohner had two more years on the gravy train. It seems to me he'd want to patch up whatever differences he had with Buford so the contract would be renewed."

"How deep was the rift between them?" MacDuff asked. He glanced at Liz and Sophie. "You had some contact with him. You were at the party. Did you pick up on anything to make you think he has a short fuse—that he could be aroused to violence?"

"Kohner didn't strike me as a man with an explosive temper," Liz replied. "I don't believe a little falling out with a client would set him off."

"Yeah, I agree," Sophie said. "And at the party he was concerned about Buford's drinking. Remember, Liz, we heard him tell Sporn they should get Buford into the hot tub while he was still able to sit up?"

"Yes. There was no sign of animosity. It was more like he was looking out for Buford."

"If he was really angry at Buford, he wouldn't have given a damn how much booze Buford swilled down," Ralph said.

MacDuff glanced around the group. "Sounds like we all agree Kohner didn't have a motive. Shall we tell him we're done questioning him and he can leave here if he wants to?"

"I'll go along with that," Ralph replied.

Sophie nodded. "Me too."

"Keeping Kohner a viable suspect would only clutter up our minds," Liz said.

Ike cast her a teasing smile. "Count me in. The last thing I need right now is a cluttered mind."

"Okay, I'll notify him," MacDuff said. He set his copy of Kohner's report aside. "But first let's get going on the music arranger."

He was filling time till the lab called with results on Pedro's fingerprint match, Liz decided, as she picked up her copy of Sporn's report. They'd already tried, without success, to come up with a reason for the music arranger to want Buford dead.

Ike looked up from checking his notes. "So far I can't think of any reason why he'd kill Buford, but we can't rule out that he could have been the person Liz saw at the icehouse at ten twenty-five. He had ample time after his interview to get over there."

Ample time to have gone out on the verandah, Liz thought. Ample time to phone his wife before rushing off in embarrassment when he realized his intimate conversation had been overheard. She'd considered the possibility that it hadn't been embarrassment that sent him rushing off, but the shock of seeing one of the women he'd locked in the cave. She'd dismissed the idea. She hadn't even mentioned it.

"There's something I should have run by you," she said, looking around the group. She told them about her encounter with Sporn on the verandah.

"I didn't tell you about this before because the idea of Sporn being the killer didn't make sense to me. It still doesn't, but I decided you should know about it."

"It doesn't make sense to me, either," Ike said. "His reputation as an arranger took off like a rocket after he started working with Buford."

"Especially after Buford wrote 'True Blue Texas Love.' His arrangement of that one helped make it a huge hit," Sophie replied.

"You'd think he'd want Buford to go on writing more songs like that," Ralph said.

"Yup," MacDuff agreed. "Seems to me he'd want to keep Buford alive for a long time." He glanced back at Sporn's report. "Neighbors say he's a quiet man, devoted to his wife."

"And his wife doesn't like him going on tour with Buford," Ralph added.

"Yes—from what I heard him saying to her on the phone, I gathered she was nagging him about that," Liz said.

"Are you sure he was talking to his wife?" Sophie asked.

"Well, he called her sweetheart and darling, and, remember, according to his neighbors, he was devoted to his wife."

"You said he was embarrassed when he realized you'd heard his end of the phone conversation," Ike said.

"Yes, his face got as red as a beet and he rushed off."

A sudden thought flashed into her mind. *Sporn's notebook!* It had been in her purse all this time! How could she have forgotten about it? Was she losing her touch for picking up possible clues? No, she told herself. Her run in with Yaker, seeing someone at the cave door, and the reports on the suspects must have driven it from her mind.

Ike and Andy might be interested in looking at the notebook, she thought, even though a connection to Buford's murder wasn't likely. As she groped in her purse for it, MacDuff's phone rang. All eyes turned to him as he answered it.

Could it be the lab? Liz asked herself. Was it possible they had results in so short a time?

When she saw MacDuff smile she knew he had the results and there'd been a match between the prints on Buford's hatband and one of the other items collected as evidence.

"Good news?" she asked, when he rang off.

"Yup," he replied. "They ran the room service dishes first. The prints lifted from the aluminum lids and the prints from the hatband are like peas in a pod."

Chapter Eighteen

For a moment nobody spoke. It was as if none of them wanted to acknowledge that the matching fingerprints were those of the genial bellman.

"Is there a chance the prints aren't Pedro's?" Liz asked.

"Yeah, those aluminum serving covers could have been handled by others in the kitchen before Pedro," Sophie said. "Someone else could have put them on the cart."

"Only one set of prints showed up on the lids," MacDuff replied.

Liz pictured the serving cart in the kitchen, being loaded. She had to admit it seemed logical that Pedro would have taken the aluminum lids out of the dishwasher or storage bin himself, and put them on the cart. He would have handed the cook the serving dishes to be filled, then brought them back to the cart and covered them. His would be the only prints on the aluminum covers.

"Where do we go from here?" she asked.

"When we question Pedro again, he might have some explanation why he had his hands on Buford's hat," MacDuff said. "I'll call the manager and ask him to send him up here for a few minutes."

While he phoned the manager, Ike called down to Mac-Duff's deputy at the elevator, telling him they were expecting Pedro. Liz, Sophie, and Ralph went to chairs on the other side of the room from where they could see Pedro and listen to the interrogation without participating in it.

A few minutes later, they heard the elevator. Pedro appeared. His ever-present smile was missing. He looked troubled.

"I know why you want talk to me," he said. "You think I let newsman wear my jacket and bring food here." He shook his head with vehemence. "I am working in dining room and don't know nothing about it till they tell me in kitchen. He steal coat from storeroom and tell cooks he new waiter and he take lunch cart to penthouse."

Liz asked herself if a man guilty of murder would believe he'd been summoned because of this incident. Wouldn't he take it for granted he was going to be questioned about Buford's death?

"It's okay, Pedro," Ike said. "We're pleased to hear you had nothing to do with it, but we didn't ask you to come up here about that. We want to ask you a few questions."

The distressed look on Pedro's face vanished into a broad smile. "Sure, I tell you anything I can. What you want to know?"

MacDuff motioned for him to be seated with them at the coffee table. "First, you delivered food here the night of the party, right?"

Pedro nodded. "China food."

"Was Buford still in the hot tub when you got here?" Ike asked.

"He get out of tub when I come," Pedro replied. He shook his head, looking sad for a moment. "Last time I see Buford, he having good time, eating China food. I hear someone say good, he need to eat—he got too many drinks."

"Did you think he looked like he'd had too much to drink?" Ike asked.

"Sure, he got plenty, all right. The guards, they have to help him out of tub."

"Was he able to walk okay?" MacDuff asked.

"He not walk so good," Pedro replied. "He fall down near bar. I help guards get him into chair."

"I guess he wasn't hurt if he was eating and having a good time afterwards," Ike said.

"It couldn't have been much of a fall," MacDuff added.

Where were Ike and Andy going with this? Liz wondered.

"No, he not fall bad," Pedro replied. "But his *sombrero,* it come off on floor by bar."

Bingo! With a feeling of triumph, Liz knew what had happened. Pedro had picked up the Stetson! The expressions on Ike's face and MacDuff's indicated they knew it, too. Sophie and Ralph looked pleased, as well. None of them wanted the likeable bellman to be the killer.

But Ike wanted to nail down exactly how Pedro had handled the Stetson. "Well, no harm done, unless the hat happened to land upside down in a spilled drink," he said, jokingly.

Pedro grinned in appreciation of the humor. "It upside down all right but it not land in drink. I pick it up and brush off top and fix band straight."

That did it! If all this had happened as Pedro said, a possible case couldn't be built against him, Liz thought.

"Well, we're done with the questions, Pedro," MacDuff said. "We'll let you get back to work."

"Thanks for being so cooperative," Ike added.

Pedro seemed reluctant to leave. Liz got the feeling he would have liked to join them in trying to figure out the killer's identity. After he'd gone, she and Sophie and Ralph went back to their chairs around the coffee table.

MacDuff picked up his phone. "I'm calling the guards to check out Pedro's story," he said. "If they back it up, we can strike him off as a suspect."

That leaves Erwin Sporn as the remaining one. With this thought, Liz remembered Sporn's notebook, still in her purse. She took it out.

"What's that?" Ike asked.

When she explained what it was and how she happened to have it, Ike's eyes lit up. "Anything interesting in it?" he asked.

"I haven't looked at it yet, but I can't imagine there'd be anything in it to do with the murder."

"Well, take a look, anyway."

"Yeah, now that it appears that Pedro and Kohner are off the list, we need to get something on Sporn," Sophie said. Evidently she'd given up suspecting Bonnie Lou.

Just as Liz opened the notebook, MacDuff finished his phone call to the guards. "Pedro's story checks out," he announced. "They both remember Pedro picking up the hat and straightening the hatband." He paused, noticing the open notebook. "What have you got there?"

"Some evidence on Sporn, we hope," Sophie replied. "He's the only one left."

Liz flipped through the first few pages of the notebook. "Don't get your hopes up. This is just a bunch of musical notes drawn in pencil. I guess he jotted them in here when he was doing arrangements."

"I don't know anything about music arranging," Ralph said. "Is that how they do it?"

"I probably know less than you," Ike replied. He looked around the group. "Would an arranger write his ideas in a small notebook like this one?"

"Why not?" Sophie asked. "Sporn probably likes to carry a small notebook around with him so he can jot down his ideas whenever they come to him."

Ike nodded. "That makes sense. He might have been doing some jotting when Liz saw him on the verandah."

"Before his wife phoned him," Liz said, with a wry smile.

Ike and Liz studied the first few pages. "The entries have dates on them," Ike said. "Looks like Sporn started keeping this notebook a long time ago."

"Check and see if there are any recent entries," MacDuff suggested.

Slowly, Liz turned the pages. "I don't see any new entries," she began. Then she came to the final page. "Oh, here's one. The last entry was made a couple of weeks ago," she said. "It must be an arrangement of a new song."

Dorothy P. O'Neill

"What about the entry before that?" Ike asked.

"It's dated over three years ago," Liz replied. "That's a long while between . . ." She stopped short when she noticed some lines scrawled in the margins and above the musical notes. "Look here," she said, pointing out the words in the three-year-old entry. "These are the lyrics to Buford's hit song."

Ike read the notation at the top of the page, aloud. "Possible title, 'True Blue Texas Love.'"

For a moment they all looked at one another in puzzlement. Liz asked herself why Sporn had the notes and lyrics of Buford's hit song written in his notebook for more than three years when Buford didn't write it till last year.

Ike had the answer. "Buford didn't write 'True Blue Texas Love,' Sporn did!" he exclaimed. He went on to explain. "Sporn didn't start arranging for Buford till two years ago. They didn't even know each other till then."

For an instant, they all stared at him. Then they all started talking.

"You got it, Ike," MacDuff said. "Buford talked Sporn into letting everyone think he'd written the song himself."

"Why would Sporn agree to that?" Ralph asked.

"Yeah," Sophie said. "It doesn't make sense."

"Maybe Buford paid him for the song," Liz suggested. That would explain Sporn's grumpiness, she thought. His report stated he'd tried writing songs for years without success. Then, the song he turned over to Buford became a huge hit, and Buford was getting all the accolades for Sporn's musical composition and lyrics. "This could be the reason why Sporn seems grouchy," she said.

"It doesn't add up," Ike replied. "If Sporn really wanted the world to know he's the one who wrote the music and lyrics to 'True Blue Texas Love,' he could easily prove it with this notebook."

"Maybe he and Buford had a legal agreement that he'd never claim he wrote it," Ralph suggested.

"If they did, Kohner would know about it," MacDuff

replied. "As Buford's manager, he'd be in on any legal matters."

"I think we should get Kohner up here for some questions," Ike said.

"Me too," Liz said. More than once Pop had told her to go with her hunches. Now she had a hunch there was something fishy about Sporn letting Buford take all the credit for the only song he ever wrote that was any good.

MacDuff pocketed the notebook, picked up his phone and called Kohner's room. The desk clerk reported no answer but said he'd have him paged.

Ike got to his feet. "Now would be a good time for a coffee break," he said, heading for the bar. "The pot's almost empty. I'll make some fresh."

Sophie looked at Liz. "What do you think about all this?"

"About the song? I think there's something strange about it."

"So do I. Sporn's hiding something."

Liz laughed. "Sounds like you're ready to scratch Bonnie Lou."

"I've already eliminated her," Sophie replied. "I got over my Polish stubbornness and told myself she's not strong enough."

"Not strong enough to grab Buford's ankles in the tub and pull him under?"

"Well, that too, but the main reason I changed my mind is the plant container. It's made of concrete and besides, it's studded all over with stones and rocks. I got to thinking about it and realized it would take a man to pick it up."

"Not so long ago I heard you say no man would bother to pick it up except someone very neat and orderly."

"Yeah, I said that. That's why I didn't go for Kohner being the one—he's such a slob."

"Am I getting vibes that you think Sporn might have picked up the plant?"

"You are. He's as compulsively neat as Kohner is a slob. When Kohner dropped those gum wrappers on the lobby floor and left them there, and Sporn picked them up and put them in a trash bin . . ."

"Hold it!" Liz said. "Sporn picked up the gum wrappers? I didn't see that."

"I wouldn't have seen it either if I hadn't glanced over my shoulder when I heard Sporn click off his phone."

Liz felt a tingle of excitement. If Sporn had indeed up-righted the fallen plant, that meant he was the one who'd fought briefly with Buford, and afterwards, when Buford got into the hot tub, dragged him underwater by the ankles and drowned him.

But what would have been his motive? Liz asked herself. Having Buford hailed as the talented composer and lyricist of "True Blue Texas Love" might have angered Sporn, but that shouldn't have been enough to commit murder. As Ike pointed out, all Sporn had to do was present proof that the song was his.

Apparently, while she and Sophie were talking, Kohner had answered the page. "Kohner's on his way up here now," MacDuff announced.

Good, Liz thought. *Maybe he'll have some answers.*

Again, she, Sophie, and Ralph seated themselves on the other side of the room, out of the way, but within earshot. Kohner arrived, wearing wrinkled shorts and a t-shirt. He'd been out on the putting green when he heard the page over the loudspeaker, he said. He seemed to be a bit short of breath, as if he'd rushed up here as fast as he could.

"Have you got news for me?" he asked. "Have you found out who . . . ?"

MacDuff broke in. "Sorry, no news. We just need to ask you a couple of questions."

"Have a seat," Ike said. "Coffee?"

"No, thanks." Kohner suddenly sounded guarded. "I've already told you everything I know."

"You've been very cooperative," Ike said, in his "good cop" tone. "But there's something we didn't cover." He glanced at MacDuff.

"As Buford's manager, were you aware of all the contracts he entered into?" MacDuff asked.

"Of course I knew of all those connected with his career," Kohner replied. His face bore a what's-this-all-about expression.

"Then I guess if Buford had a contract with Erwin Sporn other than the one in which Sporn became his music arranger, you'd know about it," MacDuff said.

"Naturally I'd know about it. There was never any other contract with Sporn. Why would there be?"

"An agreement, then. Was there an agreement between Sporn and Buford about one of Sporn's songs?"

"What songs? Erwin's one of the best arrangers in the business, but he's no composer. He tried it but never got anywhere. He gave that up long before he signed with Buford."

"Was 'True Blue Texas Love' Buford's first song?" Ike asked.

"Yes. I'll admit I was surprised. I knew the kid could strum a guitar and sing as good as Elvis, but I didn't dream he could ever write a song like that."

"Was he working on another one?" MacDuff asked.

"Yes. He didn't tell me much about it, only that it was coming along and he'd have it ready soon."

Liz recalled the last entry in Sporn's notebook, dated only two weeks ago. That had to be the song Buford said would be ready soon—as soon as Sporn finished writing it!

In another flash of memory, she recalled something Bonnie Lou had told Ike and Andy during her interview. On that fateful night, Buford had left their bedroom saying he had an idea for a new song and he wanted to stay up awhile. How did this connect with what they now knew? She shook her head in puzzlement.

"Well, thanks for your cooperation, Mr. Kohner," MacDuff said, getting to his feet. "No more questions. And you can leave the hotel any time, if you want to."

Ike stood up, too. "Thanks, Mr. Kohner. We know this is a difficult time for you."

Kohner rose. "Yes. It'll be a long time before I get over the shock. I'll be checking out in an hour or so. Good luck with your investigation."

As soon as he left, Liz, Sophie, and Ralph rushed from across the room.

"He sure as hell doesn't know Sporn wrote the song," Ralph said.

"Yup, he convinced *me,*" MacDuff replied. "What do you think, Ike?"

"Same as you. He's completely in the dark." Ike looked at Liz and Sophie.

"There's no doubt in my mind, he believes Buford composed 'True Blue Texas Love,' and wrote the lyrics, too," Liz said.

"Ditto," Sophie added.

"Now we have to figure out how this could shape into a motive for Sporn," Ike said. "Let's all sit down and throw out some ideas."

They were barely seated when Sophie spoke up. "Before we get going on ideas for a motive, I want to say I'm sure Sporn was the one who picked up the fallen plant."

Ralph chuckled. "Sophie, my love, weren't you the one who insisted it had to be a woman who picked it up? Didn't you say a man wouldn't bother to do that?"

"Yeah, but since then it struck me that Sporn is an extremely orderly man," Sophie replied. She related the incident in the lobby when Sporn picked up the gum wrappers Kohner had left on the floor.

"This ties in," MacDuff said. "We've known all along whoever picked up the plant is most likely the killer. Now let's throw out some thoughts on why Sporn would want Buford dead."

"I think it has something to do with the song," Liz said. "We all agree Sporn and Buford probably made a private agreement to let Buford say he wrote it. If we could figure out why Sporn was willing to do that . . ."

"Maybe Buford paid him a bundle," Sophie suggested.

Liz took off with this idea. "Then maybe Sporn changed

his mind and wanted to publish the song as his and said he'd give the money back, but Buford refused."

Ike shook his head. "Andy's P.I. didn't uncover any large deposits in Sporn's bank account."

"Okay," MacDuff said. "We have good evidence that Sporn wrote the hit song Buford passed off as his. We also have evidence that Sporn started another song that Buford intended to claim as his own. But there's no evidence that Sporn had objections to any of this. There's nothing here to indicate a motive for murder."

"No evidence that he objected to it, except he was grouchy all the time," Liz replied. "I think he regretted letting Buford take over his first song, and I think he wanted that new song to come out as his."

"There was nothing to keep him from claiming the first song as his, or telling Buford hands off the new song," Ike said.

There had to be *something,* Liz thought. If they could figure out what it was, they'd have their motive for the music arranger.

"Sporn and Buford must have been pretty friendly for Sporn to turn over his songs like that," Ralph said.

Ike looked dubious. "I suppose friendship could be the answer. But if it is, it complicates things."

He meant they'd have trouble finding a motive, Liz thought.

"Friendship—I'll bet that's it," Sophie replied. "Traveling around on tours together, they got to be buddies."

The idea of quiet, conservative, middle-aged, music arranger Erwin Sporn and party hound, womanizing, young rock star, Buford Doakes as buddies seemed incongruous to Liz. But it could have happened, she decided. From that overheard phone conversation, she knew Sporn wasn't happy on the road without his wife. He probably felt lonesome.

She imagined Buford trying to cheer up the lonely music arranger, talking him into bouts of drinking—even smoking a joint or two. A moment later her already ignited imagination took off like wildfire. She pictured Sporn consorting with Buford's party girls.

In a flash, all the fragments of information and imagination came together in her mind. She knew it was Erwin Sporn who'd drowned Buford and she knew why he'd done it.

Almost overcome with excitement, she slid to the edge of her chair. "Listen up, everybody," she said. "I've figured out a motive for Sporn!"

Chapter Nineteen

During the few moments of silence that followed her announcement, Liz sensed surprise, doubt, even disbelief. Just as she asked herself if her imagination had carried her too far, Ike spoke.

"Liz doesn't make statements like that without good reason. I'd be willing to bet my last buck that she's latched onto something."

As she smiled her thanks, he returned the smile, adding, "Go ahead, let's hear what you've come up with."

She felt confident her latest idea would justify his faith in her sleuthing ability. "In Sporn's background report, neighbors described him as a devoted husband," she began. "I think that's an understatement. After hearing him talk to his wife on the phone, I think he's crazy in love with her."

"It must be vice versa," Sophie replied. "His report said she didn't like it that she couldn't go along on concert tours with him."

Liz nodded. "And from the phone conversation I overheard, I gathered he had to reassure her, constantly, that he didn't enjoy going on tours without her."

"Hey, I think I get it," Sophie said. "She thought he might be playing around while he was on tour."

"Exactly," Liz replied.

"Well *I* don't get it," Ralph said. "Neighbors said he was a devoted husband."

"Even a devoted husband might stray if he were plied with enough booze and pot," Liz said.

Ralph looked at her in puzzlement. "What gave you that idea?"

"You and Sophie did, when you said that Sporn and Buford must have become good friends, going on so many tours together. I believe Buford knew Sporn was lonesome and decided to cheer him up . . ."

"You think Buford got his lonesome pal Sporn partying with him and his female fans?" MacDuff asked.

"I think it might have happened just once," Liz replied. "And Sporn was terrified his wife would find out. I think Sporn had shown Buford the music and lyrics of 'True Blue Texas Love' and Buford had recognized its potential. I think he told Sporn he'd keep mum about the transgression if Sporn would let him bring out the song as his own."

She paused, looking around the group. "Sporn agreed," she continued, "but when Buford found out Sporn was writing another song, he insisted on having that one too, and threatened to spill the beans if Sporn didn't comply."

"Blackmail!" Ike exclaimed, "After years of trying, Sporn knew he'd finally mastered the technique of successful songwriting. He was looking forward to writing hits as big as 'True Blue Texas Love' and being acclaimed as a talented composer. But when Buford demanded the second song, Sporn realized there'd be no end to it."

MacDuff nodded. "To preserve his marriage, he'd be forced to turn over anything he wrote to Buford."

"We need to let Sporn know we have his notebook and question him," Ike said. He leaned over and gave Liz a hug. "Congratulations, you've given us our motive."

The look in his eyes wasn't merely an expression of admiration for her sleuthing talents. Seeing it made her want to be alone with him. It had been too long.

"Hearing the motive explained, it seems so clear I wonder

why I didn't think of it myself," Ralph said. "Guess I couldn't picture Sporn killing anyone for any reason."

"That's because he comes across as a harmless wimp," Sophie replied.

"Blackmail can turn the most unlikely people into killers," MacDuff said.

Ike nodded in agreement. "It drove Sporn to desperation."

"I might feel sorry for him if he hadn't locked us in the cave," Sophie said.

"That was part of his desperation," Liz said. "I'm sure, now, he thought we were New York detectives. That was his chance to get us out of the way during the interviews."

"Yeah? Well I'm not sure he'd ever have let us out," Sophie replied.

"There's something we haven't covered," Ralph said. "How did Sporn get into the penthouse when he didn't have a key?"

Liz looked at MacDuff and then at Ike. She had her own ideas about how Sporn got into the penthouse without a key, but she was sure they'd figured it out. She waited for one of them to explain.

"Buford let him in," Ike replied. "You remember Bonnie Lou told us Buford left the bedroom after telling her he had an idea for a song and he wanted to work on it? He must have decided to tell Sporn, that night, that he was taking over the new song. He phoned Sporn to come up to the penthouse."

"And that's when Sporn realized he was being blackmailed," MacDuff said.

Liz glanced across the room where the array of plants stood along the side of the hot tub. Again, she pictured the plant being knocked over during a fight between Buford and his killer. Only this time the killer in the picture wasn't a shadowy non-person struggling with Buford for some reason unknown to her. He was a real flesh and blood man—a man driven to desperation, doing whatever it took to keep his wife from knowing he'd been unfaithful.

"Do we have enough on Sporn for an arrest?" she asked.

MacDuff looked at Ike. "I haven't had the experience

with homicides that you have, but I don't think we have enough to go on."

"You're absolutely right," Ike replied. "With what we have, I wouldn't want to try it."

They needed some physical evidence that Sporn had been in the penthouse after the party ended, Liz thought. Evidence that Sporn had been in a fight last night might help. She thought, again, of middle-aged, sparely-built Sporn pitted against young, muscular Buford. "Did you notice any bruises on Sporn's face when you interviewed him this morning?" she asked.

"No," Ike replied. "But that's not surprising. Buford wasn't in the best shape for a fist fight."

"There were minor red marks on Buford's face," MacDuff said. "Assuming it was Sporn who dealt the blows, he got in his licks and dodged Buford every time. During the interviews I checked out the knuckles of all the men and found no abrasions. Evidently Buford wasn't hit very hard. As it stands now, there's no proof that Sporn came back to the penthouse after the party ended and fought with Buford."

Liz glanced at her watch. Was there any chance of getting proof before they had to leave?

MacDuff's next statement didn't offer much hope. "Unless we come up with physical evidence that Sporn was in the penthouse after Bonnie Lou and the guards went to bed, and that he fought with Buford, we don't have enough to build a case."

Sophie sighed. "His fingerprints on Buford's Stetson would have been perfect."

"Or on that uprighted plant container," Liz added, glancing toward the stone-studded pots around the hot tub.

"We'll get Sporn on tape when we question him," Ike said. "He might let something slip."

There was a chance he might, Liz thought. She had no doubt that Sporn was the killer, but he wasn't a hardened criminal. She hoped this would make him vulnerable to Ike's skilled interrogation.

MacDuff located Sporn by telephone and asked him to

come up to the penthouse. He notified the deputy at the elevator. They all settled down to wait.

Again, Liz, Sophie, and Ralph made themselves inconspicuous on the opposite side of the spacious room. Seated in high-backed chairs turned away from the bar area, they could follow the interrogation without Sporn realizing they were there.

They heard the elevator. Liz peeked around the side of her chair. Sporn came into the room, dressed in neatly pressed dark blue slacks, light blue shirt and well-polished brown leather loafers. This morning on the verandah he'd been wearing tan slacks, white shirt and white athletic shoes, she recalled. She was surprised that he didn't look as worried as she'd expected. Except for a furtive, slightly troubled glance toward the hot tub, he gave no indication that he felt uncomfortable at the scene of his crime. Was he confident he'd gotten away with murder?

"Have a seat, Sporn," MacDuff said.

"I guess you called me up here to tell me I can check out," Sporn said, sitting down on the couch.

He *did* think he'd gotten away with it, Liz decided. He believed he'd put an end to this threat to his marriage. He was looking forward to rejoining his wife, never having to go on tour again, and being acclaimed as the composer of his future songs.

"No, we didn't ask you here to inform you you could check out," Ike said.

Liz couldn't see Sporn's face, but she guessed he'd frowned. "No? I was talking to Sid Kohner a little while ago and he said he'd been up here and you told him he could check out. Naturally, I assumed . . ." At that moment his cell phone sounded.

"If you'll excuse me . . ." Sporn said. Liz couldn't hear his muffled voice, but she was sure the caller was his wife with a rerun of what she'd overheard this morning. The woman had him tied up emotionally, she decided, like Bette Davis had Leslie Howard in that old movie, *Of Human Bondage.*

"I'm sorry for the interruption," Sporn said, as he hung

up. Liz pictured his face as it always looked after a conversation with his wife—harassed and unhappy. "So why am I here?" he asked.

The enormity of his predicament hadn't sunk in, Liz thought. It was as if he'd shut off the realization that he'd committed murder. A shrink might say he was in denial.

"We need to ask you a few questions," MacDuff said. "You don't have to answer them if you don't want to and you can leave any time you wish. But first, we have something we believe belongs to you."

Liz ventured another peek around the side of her chair. She saw MacDuff take Sporn's notebook out of his pocket and put it on the table.

As she ducked back, she heard Sporn's voice, shrill with surprise and apprehension. "Where did you get that?"

"It was found on the verandah," MacDuff replied. "There's no name in it, but when we saw the notes and words to 'True Blue Texas Love,' we knew it must be yours."

After a long pause, Sporn replied, "It's not mine. It's probably Buford's." Liz detected a quiver in his voice as he added, "He wrote the song, not me."

"You and Buford got to be good friends after a few tours together, didn't you?" Ike asked.

Liz couldn't hear Sporn's reply. She decided he must have nodded his head.

Ike pressed on. "You took the job as Buford's music arranger about two years ago—right?"

"That's right," Sporn replied.

"And prior to that you'd never met him?"

"No."

"So it was during the past two years, while you and Buford were traveling around on tours, that you became friends?" Ike asked.

"Yes . . ." Sporn's voice sounded hesitant and uncertain, Liz thought.

"Do you know when Buford wrote the music and lyrics to 'True Blue Texas Love'?" MacDuff asked.

Liz heard Sporn's voice, uncertain again. "I think it was last year."

"After you became his arranger?" MacDuff asked.

"Yes . . ."

Liz held her breath. Now might be the time for the big question.

It was, and Ike posed it. "You say Buford wrote 'True Blue Texas Love' after you became his arranger, two years ago. Can you explain the date in the notebook indicating the song was in the works more than three years ago?"

The silence following the question was so lengthy that Liz wondered if Sporn could possibly have passed out from shock. She took a peek around the side of her chair again, just as Sporn made a halting reply.

"I . . . I don't know . . . Well, yes, I can explain . . . I must have put down the wrong date . . ."

"But you told us this isn't your notebook," MacDuff reminded him.

"You said it's Buford's," Ike added.

"I . . . I meant to say *Buford* wrote the wrong date. . . ." Sporn's voice was shaky and barely audible.

Ike spoke in his best "good cop" manner. "Mr. Sporn, you composed 'True Blue Texas Love' yourself, didn't you?"

Liz heard a muffled "yes."

"There's nothing wrong with letting a friend take credit for a song you wrote yourself," Ike continued. "It was extremely generous of you."

"Yup, it sure was," MacDuff said. "You and your wife would have been sitting pretty on the money you'd have made from that hit song. But it beats me why you were planning to let Buford take over your next song, too."

Whether motivated by the mention of his wife or his new song, Sporn replied with sudden spirit. "You have that wrong. I told him I wasn't going to give him any more songs, but then he said if I didn't . . ." Apparently realizing he'd spoken too quickly and said too much, he stopped short. Liz pictured his face, etched with apprehension.

"Are you saying Buford threatened you in some way?" Ike asked.

When Liz didn't hear Sporn reply, she stole a glance around the back of the chair, again. She saw him slumped over, with his hands covering his face.

For a few optimistic moments, she believed he might be on the verge of making a confession. Perhaps the thought of his wife finding out about his infidelity stopped him. Perhaps he believed there might still be a chance of keeping this from her. Whatever his reason, he raised his head and, in a quavery voice, spoke the words often next best to an admission of guilt.

"I want to contact my attorney."

Chapter Twenty

"Certainly." Ike's voice held a restrained note of triumph. "You can put in the call from here."

Liz thought she knew why Ike seemed to have a mixed reaction to Sporn's request for an attorney. The request suggested Sporn knew he'd been caught with a motive for Buford's murder. On the other hand, with no evidence that Sporn had returned to the penthouse after the guards and Bonnie Lou had retired, Ike knew a smart lawyer might blow the idea of blackmail away like a puff of smoke.

"Yes . . . all right . . ." Sporn's voice sounded shaky. "But first I want to talk to Sid and tell him . . ." His voice trailed off, as if he didn't know exactly what he intended to tell Kohner.

Sporn might be a genius at putting music together, but when it came to murder and cover-up, he was a complete idiot, Liz thought. In all the homicides she'd followed, she'd never come across a killer with such faulty reasoning.

"Sure, phone him," MacDuff said. "He's probably in his room, packing to leave."

Sporn made the call. "Sid . . . It's me, Erwin. I . . . I'm in the penthouse with the detectives. . . Sid . . . I think I should . . . I need to get hold of Harry Glick . . ."

Apparently Kohner asked to speak to MacDuff and demanded an explanation. Within a short time, MacDuff passed him through the deputy at the elevator and he arrived in the penthouse, blustering with incredulity and indignation.

"I can't believe this. You gotta be out of your minds. Erwin, did they read you your rights?"

MacDuff broke in. "I told you on the phone, Mr. Sporn is not under arrest. We just asked him a few questions, that's all. We informed him he didn't have to answer them if he didn't want to, and he was free to leave if he wished."

"Is that right, Erwin?" Kohner asked.

Sporn's voice could barely be heard. "Yes."

"Then why didn't you tell them to shove their questions? Why in hell didn't you leave, instead of . . ." Kohner paused, apparently struck with another thought. "What kind of questions did they ask you that got you thinking you needed an attorney?"

Without waiting for an answer, he continued, evidently directing his remarks at Ike and MacDuff. "This is ridiculous. You're crazy if you think Erwin knows anything about Buford's drowning. You said he isn't under arrest and he's free to go, so come on, Erwin, let's get the hell out of here."

Liz felt a jolt of apprehension. "Can they do that?" she whispered.

"I don't think so," Sophie whispered in return. "Seems to me there's enough evidence for Sporn to be held in temporary detention."

"While the investigation continues," Ralph added.

MacDuff's reply to Kohner's outburst dispelled Liz's uncertainty. "Sorry, Mr. Kohner," he said. "Mr. Sporn is no longer free to leave. After questioning him, we . . ."

"What?" Kohner sputtered. "You're arresting him after all? Is that it? Well, we'll see about that. Don't worry, Erwin, I'm not leaving yet. I got in touch with Harry. He's on his way. He'll be here in a couple of hours and will straighten everything out."

"Mr. Sporn is not under arrest," MacDuff replied.

In the short pause that followed this announcement, Liz thought, Andy must have glanced at Ike, with a signal for him to take over.

Ike's statement was brief. "Mr. Sporn's answers to our questions and his request for an attorney warrant his detention while we continue our investigation."

"Detention—what the hell does that mean?" Kohner snarled. "Are you going to lock him up somewhere?"

"He'll be confined to the inn," Ike replied. "Sheriff Mac-Duff will assign a deputy to him."

During this talk Sporn had been silent. Now Liz stole another peek and saw him glance over at the hot tub. He looked troubled. His voice quivered as he asked, "Can I go to my room now?"

Liz got the feeling he'd been struck with a sudden need to get away from the crime scene. Had reality at last caught up with his far-out mind?

"We need you to stay awhile," MacDuff replied. "But you go ahead, Mr. Kohner."

"All right." Kohner sounded somewhat subdued. "Erwin, of course I'm sticking around till Harry gets here and clears up this mess. Phone me when you can."

After Kohner left, MacDuff picked up the phone to contact another deputy to guard Sporn. At the same time, he signaled Liz, Sophie, and Ralph to return to their places around the coffee table.

As Liz seated herself on the sofa, she again noticed that Sporn was not wearing the same clothes he'd had on when he rushed off the verandah that morning. Only a compulsive neatnik would change into dressier clothes for the afternoon, she thought.

She took special note of Sporn's reaction when she and Sophie sat down on the couch. There was no mistaking his feelings when he saw them. Even though he knew from the episode on the verandah that the two women he'd locked in the cave had escaped, their sudden, unexpected appearance here caused a look of startled guilt to spread all over his face. That was why MacDuff wanted them to sit down with him, she decided. He, too, wanted to see Sporn's reaction.

What now? Liz asked herself. Sporn had already been asked all the pertinent questions. Then it struck her that he hadn't been questioned about his whereabouts between ten and ten-thirty that morning.

Almost as if her thoughts had communicated with Ike's, she heard Ike's voice. "Mr. Sporn, you were on the verandah at ten o'clock this morning, and when you left, you accidentally dropped a notebook. And it's yours, not Buford's. Right?"

After a slight hesitation, Sporn answered. "That's right." He stole a look at Liz. She guessed he was thinking she must be the one who'd found it.

"Am I going to get it back?" he asked. Coming from a highly gifted man, the question seemed almost childlike, Liz thought.

"Sorry, we'll have to keep it for awhile," MacDuff replied.

If Sporn were going to protest, Ike's next question would have stopped him. "Where did you go after you left the verandah?"

"I . . . I went for a walk," Sporn replied.

His face was wide open to his feelings, Liz thought. He'd never win at poker.

"Lots of places to walk around here," MacDuff said. "Whereabouts did you go?"

When Sporn did not answer right away, Ike broke in. "Did you take the lakeside trail?"

"Along the lake, yes," Sporn replied.

"I've heard that's a good place to walk," Ike said. He put on a warm smile. "Very pretty. Nice view of the lake."

Ike's friendly manner wouldn't have fooled a clever killer, Liz thought. But apparently Sporn's highly creative intellect was beyond thinking such things through. She could see the tense look on his face relax. He had no idea where this was leading.

"I've also heard there are some old icehouses around there," Ike continued. "Did you happen to see any?"

Liz looked at Ike in surprise. He'd said this interview with Sporn would be taped and she'd seen him set up the recorder on the bar. Wouldn't his question give Sporn the chance to wriggle free? He could say he'd noticed the cave and decided to check it out. That would make his presence there seem like normal curiosity and end any attempts to link it with locking up two supposed detectives. She held her breath, waiting for Sporn's reply.

He answered promptly. "No . . . no, I didn't notice any old icehouses."

Good! Liz thought. If Ike could prove Sporn had lied, that would help build the case. But how would he do that? Could Sporn's shoeprints be lifted from the earth around the cave door? She knew the procedure of making plaster casts of prints on the ground was a common and often successful procedure. Ike and Andy must have thought of this.

"Okay, Mr. Sporn, I guess that's all for now," Ike said.

"The deputy will be here pretty soon," MacDuff added. "Have some coffee while you're waiting."

"Thank you." Sporn's voice sounded slightly relieved, as if he thought the end of the questioning and the offer of coffee meant he wasn't in too much trouble. It was as if his mind couldn't relate to the crime he'd committed, Liz thought.

While watching him pour his coffee, another thought popped into Liz's mind. The prints of her boots and Sophie's would be on the ground outside the cave door. She recalled how they'd danced around, hugging each other after they'd crawled out. Would Sporn's shoeprints show up clearly in a cast of the area?

She wished the deputy would arrive and take Sporn downstairs so they could discuss this and resume swapping ideas. Besides, it was awkward, sitting around the table with the man who'd locked them in the cave, even though he didn't realize they were pretty sure he was the one. She glanced at Sophie, knowing she felt uncomfortable, too. If she were Sophie she might not be able to restrain herself from mouthing off at the person who'd put her in the grip of her phobias.

The sound of the elevator told them the deputy had arrived. He was wearing a uniform. MacDuff introduced him.

"Mr. Sporn, Pete will be your constant companion until further notice," he said. "You can move freely around the inn premises but he'll always be close by."

Apparently the uniform had thrown Sporn into confusion. "I don't quite understand," Sporn said. "You said I'm not under arrest."

"You're not," MacDuff replied. "Like we said before— you're being detained temporarily while we go on with the investigation."

Andy knew correct investigative procedures as well as Ike did, Liz thought. No chance of Sporn's attorney claiming he hadn't been informed of his rights. No chance of what evidence they had being ruled inadmissible.

As soon as Sporn and the deputy left, Liz broached the subject of plaster casting Sporn's shoeprints.

"That's been done," MacDuff replied. "Unfortunately, the ground around the cave was too roughed up with other prints to get a clear impression."

"While Sporn was here, I thought of examining his shoes for traces of dirt we could match up with the dirt outside the cave," Ike said. "But did you notice those loafers? They looked like they just walked out of a shoe store."

"Yup—not a speck on them," MacDuff agreed.

"Someone as persnickety as Sporn would have given them the old spit and polish after he came back from inspecting the cave site," Sophie said.

"Or he could have changed his shoes," Ike said.

Liz nodded. "And a neat guy like him, back from a walk in the woods, wouldn't just clean or change his shoes—he'd change clothes from head to toe, and he did. On the verandah this morning, he had on different clothing and white athletic shoes."

"We should take a look at those white athletics," MacDuff said, removing a couple of evidence bags from his carrying case. "I'll phone Sporn's room. If he's there, I'll ask for permission to check out his shoes. If he refuses, we'll get a warrant."

Liz had strong hopes that Sporn's gifted mind was too far out of the loop to grasp the significance of the shoe examination.

"Ralph, how about coming with us?" Ike asked.

"Sure," Ralph replied.

MacDuff got off the phone saying Sporn was in his room and had agreed to the shoe appraisal. Moments later, the three men headed for the elevator.

"I hope Mr. Tidy Toes didn't get around to cleaning the shoes he wore to the cave this morning," Sophie called after them.

She and Liz poured coffee and settled down on the sofa.

"You said Sporn had on white athletics this morning?" Sophie asked.

"Yes," Liz replied. "The kind that have big grooves and ridges on the bottom."

"Good," Sophie said. "I noticed the trees around the cave are mostly oak. That means the soil on the ground outside the cave is very acid from oak leaves falling on it over the years. As I recall, there were mostly maples and pines along the trail and the soil would be more alkaline. If the tests show highly acidic soil stuck in the grooves of Sporn's shoes, we can be pretty sure it came from the area around the cave."

"I forgot you majored in biology," Liz replied, with a grin.

Sophie returned the grin. "I'd almost forgotten it, myself. This is the first time I've had the chance to use it in my police career."

"Even if Sporn cleaned his shoes after coming back from the cave, he wouldn't get every last speck out of the grooves," Liz said.

Sophie nodded. "I'll bet this will prove he was the one you saw."

They shouldn't get too excited about this latest development, Liz thought. The soil test would prove that Sporn had been nosing around the icehouse door and the fact that he'd lied would prove he was hiding something. But, like all the evidence they had, it was circumstantial. To build a solid case, they needed physical evidence.

Still, what they had was a collection of small bits of evidence. If they could only prove that Sporn had returned to the penthouse late on that fateful night, all the smaller bits would fit around that proof, like the pieces of an intricate mosaic. They'd have a case the craftiest criminal defense attorney couldn't blast.

"Let's go over what we know about Sporn," she suggested. "First, we know he's a gifted music arranger, crazy about a wife who phones him around the clock. He's a henpecked genius."

"A henpecked genius—good one," Sophie said, smiling in appreciation. "And we know he wrote the music and lyrics to 'True Blue Texas Love' and let Buford take credit as the composer."

"Right," Liz said. "And he did it so Buford wouldn't spill the beans to his wife about the partying that got out of hand."

"Yeah, and we know Sporn was working on a new song and Buford found out about it."

"And we're pretty sure Buford phoned Sporn to come up to the penthouse that night, after everyone else was asleep," Liz replied, "That's when he must have told Sporn he wanted the new song."

"Then, when Sporn refused, Buford threatened to let the wife know about the extramarital misstep," Sophie said.

Liz nodded. "That's when Sporn lost it and started swinging at Buford. We know he landed at least one punch—Andy said there were red marks on Buford's face. Buford probably tried to return the blows but he was too stoned and drunk to connect. The way I see it, after the plant was knocked over, Buford decided to quit the fight. He got into the hot tub, thinking that would end it. I can imagine him lolling in the water, floating his legs and feet . . ."

"And making taunting remarks," Sophie said. "Maybe mentioning Sporn's wife."

"Oh, yes, I can almost hear him," Liz replied. "Sporn was still fighting mad, and the taunts drove him into a rage."

"So, in a fury, he rushed over to the hot tub and grabbed Buford by the ankles, and dragged him under," Sophie concluded.

"Do you think he picked up the overturned plant before or after he drowned Buford?" Liz asked.

"I think it was after," Sophie replied. "He was in too much of a rage to do it beforehand. All he was thinking of was silencing Buford."

"I know he's compulsively neat, but when he realized Buford wasn't coming up for air, don't you think he would have wanted to get out of there as fast as he could?"

"Well, maybe. But it doesn't matter when he picked up the plant," Sophie said. "We know he did, and if the damn pot wasn't made of concrete and stones, his fingerprints could be lifted and the case would be sewn up."

At that moment Sophie's phone sounded. "It's Ralph," she said, glancing at the caller ID. Moments later, she broke into a big smile. "They found the athletic shoes and they have black dirt on them," she announced, as she clicked off the phone. "Andy's having someone get a sample of the dirt around the cave and sending it to the lab with the shoes. And Ralph said he and Ike will be back here in a few minutes."

Chapter Twenty-one

"Andy's meeting with the reporters. He'll be here shortly," Ike said, as he and Ralph came into the penthouse.

"Is he going to make a statement about Sporn?" Liz asked.

"He's going to tell them we're close to making an arrest, but he's not revealing the name yet."

Ike and Ralph headed for the coffeemaker. Liz waited till they'd filled their mugs and settled into chairs before posing her question. "Is Andy making his statement to the news media because of the dirt found on Sporn's shoes?"

"Not entirely," Ike replied. "On the strength of everything we have on Sporn, I advised Andy to go ahead and make the statement. After what the governor said on TV, I thought Andy should set the record straight. He's been working hard on the case and there's been considerable progress."

It was true, they'd come a long way from the original seven suspects, Liz thought. Andy's statement to the media would keep the public from believing that the investigation was at a standstill because of an inept country bumpkin of a sheriff.

"I know you believe we need proof that Sporn went back to the penthouse," she said. "But when I think of where we started and where we are now . . . couldn't there be an arrest without it?"

"That's up to Andy," Ike replied. "But as it stands now, I wouldn't do it."

The much-needed physical evidence, Liz thought, with a sigh. The stumbling block on an otherwise clear path.

Her thoughts returned to the incriminating athletic shoes. "How did Sporn react when you told him you were there to look over his shoes?" she asked.

"At first he didn't have much of a reaction," Ike replied. "It was as if he didn't connect his shoes to where he'd been that morning."

Another indication that Sporn's mind was on a different planet, Liz thought.

"Luckily, he hadn't cleaned his athletic shoes yet," Ike went on. "When he saw us examining them, it must have suddenly dawned on him he'd had them on when he went to the cave."

"Then he told us he hadn't worn them since he arrived at the inn," Ralph said.

Sophie gave a snort of laughter. "Like he'd pack a pair of dirty shoes."

Ike glanced at his watch. "It's getting close to check-out time. While we're waiting for Andy, let's get packed and go down to the desk. After we've signed out we can take our bags to the cars and then come back up here. We can hang out and work on the case till it's time to hit the road."

"Sophie and I can pack and check out now, but you guys better stay here in case Andy comes back," Liz said. "You can go down after he gets here."

"Right, we don't want Andy to come up to an empty penthouse and think we've all walked out on him," Ralph said.

"Like rats deserting a sinking ship," Sophie added. The instant the words were spoken, she clapped her hand over her mouth. "Oh, I don't know why I said that! Please pretend you didn't hear it."

"Hear what?" Ike asked.

Ralph grinned at her. "Did you say something, sweetheart?"

"I was thinking of something else and didn't get it," Liz said.

"Thanks, you liars," Sophie replied. "Cross my heart, I don't think this case is going under. I haven't given up on finding something that will prove Sporn came back here that night."

MacDuff walked into the room just in time to catch Sophie's last few words. "I haven't given up, either," he said. "We're all smart folks or we wouldn't have gotten as much as we have on Sporn. In the three, maybe four hours before you have to head for home, we should be able to nail down the evidence we need."

The optimistic statement seemed to energize Ike. "We can do it if we concentrate," he replied. "Let's all check out and put our bags in the cars, then come back up here ready to swing into action."

Since it was still a bit early for checking out, the lobby was almost empty and the desk clerk not busy.

"Thank goodness we didn't run into the Lexus guys or Gail," Sophie said, as they took the elevator back up to the penthouse. "It would have been nice to say good-bye, but they'd have asked us a million questions."

"Right," Liz replied. "We'd have been drawn into a lengthy discussion."

"We don't have time for that. We need to get to work," Ike said.

They were like racers coming down to the wire, Liz thought—all determined to make one last spurt of effort.

Back in the penthouse, they seated themselves around the table.

"We should focus on any possible areas where Sporn could have left his fingerprints when he came back to the penthouse," Ike said. "The tub area hasn't been dusted yet, but you've got a dusting kit here, right, Andy?"

"Yup. And the glass from Sporn's bathroom is in the lab, ready to be matched."

Ike glanced toward the hot tub. "We believe most of the

action prior to the murder took place around the tub. Liz, when you and Sophie were at the party, did you notice if Sporn went over there?"

Liz shook her head. "I didn't see him near the hot tub, did you Sophie?"

"No. While we were there I never saw him leave the bar area."

"But didn't you mention that he and Kohner talked about getting Buford into the tub before he got too drunk?"

"Yeah, but neither of them helped him into the tub. We saw the guards do it," Sophie replied.

"Sporn could have gone over to watch the action in the hot tub after you and Liz left the party," Ralph said.

Liz shook her head, "From what I've learned about him, he wouldn't hang around ogling women in bikinis. He probably spent the whole time on the phone with his wife."

"Okay, so let's say Sporn didn't go near the hot tub while he was at the party," MacDuff said. "And, according to the guards, neither Kohner nor Sporn were in the penthouse prior to the party. If we pick up Sporn's prints around the tub, that could mean he came back after the party was over."

"We need to think of someplace around the tub where he might have placed his hands or something he might have grabbed or touched," Ike said. He rose from his chair. "Let's go over there and see if we can come up with some ideas."

As they walked across the room toward the hot tub, Liz pictured the fight between Buford and Sporn. If Sporn's fingerprints were anywhere in that area, where would they be?

She studied the tub's surroundings—a row of windows on one side, plants on the other, a section of wall at each end. Maybe, while they were struggling, Sporn pushed Buford against one of those walls, she thought. Maybe one of Sporn's hands smacked against the wall. She expressed this possibility aloud.

"We'll give the walls a dusting and see what we get," MacDuff said.

"What about the top side of the tub in the corner where Buford was found?" Sophie asked. "If Sporn crouched or knelt before reaching in to grab Buford's ankles, maybe he put his hands down to brace himself."

"With all those women getting into the water, there'll be multiple prints there, and the area might have been wet, too, but we'll dust and see," MacDuff replied.

While Ike and MacDuff tested for prints, Liz, Sophie, and Ralph continued looking around. The tub area was devoid of furnishings. Except for the section of tiled floor, there was no other surface that would hold fingerprints, Liz noticed. But even her vivid imagination couldn't quite picture Sporn pinning Buford to the floor and leaving fingerprints on the tiles. She decided to mention it to Ralph, anyway. Being male, and a cop, he might know if this could happen in a fight.

Ralph pondered this. "Prints on the tile floor while they were fighting? Yeah, I think it could happen."

Suddenly he looked as if another possibility had struck him. "What if some of the fighting took place on the carpet!" he exclaimed. "We've been concentrating on fingerprints, but what about fibers from Sporn's clothing?"

"Andy's way ahead on the fibers," Ike said, as he and MacDuff walked over from where they'd been working. "He had that attended to early on."

"Just routine," MacDuff said.

"I should have known that wouldn't get by you, Andy," Ralph said.

Sophie shook her head. "I don't think they were fighting on the floor. If the fight got that heavy, wouldn't they have made enough noise to wake up the guards?"

"Probably," MacDuff replied. "But we have to consider every possibility. If we don't find any other physical evidence today, I'll have Sporn's clothing tested for carpet fibers. And getting back to fibers on the carpet, we picked up some polyester and nylon. I figured some of the women at the party were wearing nylon or polyester and they might have sat on the floor—maybe while they were wearing their bikinis."

He looked at Liz and Sophie. "Like I said, we can't overlook any possibility. Women are better at noticing clothing details than men are. Generally speaking, what did you notice about the way Sporn dresses?"

"I don't think he's a polyester kind of guy," Sophie replied. "When he was up here before he had on dark blue slacks that looked like lightweight wool flannel and a blue shirt that definitely wasn't a synthetic fabric. He's a classy dresser, right, Liz?"

Liz nodded. "Right—too classy to wear polyester slacks. And every time we saw him he had on an expensive-looking shirt—like Egyptian cotton." Remembering Sporn's paisley cravat, she described it, adding, "I could tell it was pure silk."

"He must have been asleep when Buford phoned him. He wouldn't have put on anything fancy. Maybe he didn't bother to get fully dressed and came up here in nylon pajamas or something," MacDuff said.

Liz shook her head. "Sophie and I have never seen him wearing anything that looked like it was made of synthetics. Maybe he's allergic to man-made fabric or material. Did you notice even his athletic shoes were leather?"

MacDuff nodded. "Yup, I did. Well, I'm satisfied that those nylon and polyester threads on the carpet didn't come from Sporn's clothing."

"Did you lift any prints from the walls?" Ralph asked.

"Nope, not a one. And the side of the tub was too much of a mish mash."

Ike smiled at Liz. "So that leaves the tile floor." The smile and the brief comment conveyed a heartening message. He approved of her idea. Now, if she could only accomplish what she had in past cases and hear him say, "You've done it again, Liz."

She watched the tile floor being dusted. Would this be it? she asked herself. If not, the quest for physical evidence would come to a dead end. To ease her suspense, she walked around the room. She was standing at the windows, watching sailboats skimming over the lake, when Sophie joined her.

They both glanced toward Ike, MacDuff, and Ralph,

who'd pitched in on dusting the tiles. Liz didn't hear any comments or notice any signs of encouragement on their faces. That could only mean they hadn't found anything yet.

"Do you think Andy would go ahead and arrest Sporn without proof that he was up here after the party ended?" Liz asked.

"Maybe, but I agree with Ike—a hotshot defense attorney could rip our circumstantial evidence apart," Sophie replied.

They walked back to the tub area. Through the cluster of tall plants, they watched the dusting procedure.

"How's it going?" Liz called.

Ike's voice sounded discouraged. "Nothing. We're almost ready to call it quits."

With a sigh, Liz glanced at the plant standing slightly apart from the others. How frustrating that its stone-and-rock-studded container, apparently the one object Sporn had handled when he returned to the penthouse that night, wouldn't hold fingerprints.

She stepped closer to the plant. The sight of its broad, variegated leaves stirred her memory. *Mom used to have one just like it.* She'd kept it in the bay window of the dining room in their Staten Island house. Liz recalled it used to drop a leaf or two now and then for no apparent reason. Whenever Mom asked her to water it, she'd always say, "Be careful."

At that moment, something clicked in her mind. If this species of plant was prone to losing leaves while sitting quietly in a window, wouldn't this particular one have lost a couple when it was knocked over onto the floor?

And when Sporn picked up the container, wouldn't he also have picked up any fallen leaves?

She trembled with excitement, believing she knew the answer even before she looked down into the container. There, well below the rim, in the shadowed soil at the base of the plant, lay three leaves.

"Ike! Andy!" she called. "Please tell me that fingerprints can be lifted from live plants!"

Chapter Twenty-two

"Absolutely," Ike said. Andy added a characteristic "yup."

Seconds after these laconic replies, they must have realized she was standing next to the plant Sporn had picked up and she was staring down into the container. The full impact of her question hit them.

Ike was at her side in an instant, with Andy and Ralph on his heels. It took a moment for them to see the leaves down in the deep container, but when they did she knew she'd never forget the excitement. Andy swept her up into a hug even before Ike did. Hugs were exchanged all around.

"Liz, you've done it again," Ike said.

She still felt stunned by her discovery. "Oh, I hope so," she replied. "But what if the leaves don't have any prints on them?"

"Yeah, like Sporn was wearing gloves when he picked them up," Sophie said.

From then on, things went into high gear. Andy took off for the police lab in Stroutsboro, with the leaves in an evidence bag, saying he had to handle this himself. "I want the tests run and the prints matched, immediately," he said. "Stay put. I won't be long. As soon as I have the results I'll notify the District Attorney. Then I'll come back here, and have Sporn taken into custody."

The District Attorney was going to be one happy guy, Liz thought. Most likely he'd been taking the heat from the governor, the same as Andy.

After MacDuff left, Ike turned on the TV. "Maybe the tape of Andy's press conference will be on," he said.

It was. Making his announcement of an impending arrest, and fielding questions from reporters, Andy came across as a capable lawman, Liz thought. She hoped the governor was watching.

"Is it true you called in a team of New York detectives to take over your investigation?" a reporter asked.

"Not true," MacDuff replied. "But it *is* true I had help from an old friend, a guest at the inn, who's a New York City police detective, plus two NYPD police officers and a very smart civilian lady, all guests here. Without their input, I wouldn't be telling you, right now, that I'm close to making an arrest. It would have taken much longer."

That should head off any attempts by Bulbous Nose to get his slanderous article published, Liz decided.

"Andy handled that very well," Ike said.

He handled the rest of his session with the news media well, too, Liz thought, when it ended. The reporters seemed satisfied. They should be. Except for a short break when he went home to eat and catch a few Z's Andy had been working on the case since four A.M. yesterday.

"Andy's home life is taking a beating this weekend," she said. "His wife must be very understanding."

"He's not married," Ike said.

Liz had a comment on the tip of her tongue—the women around here must be crazy, leaving a guy like Andy on the loose. She left it unsaid, reminding herself that, technically, Ike was on the loose, too.

"Does he have any family in the vicinity?" she asked.

"Yeah, his folks still live on the farm where he was raised. He has an apartment in Bucksville."

"It isn't often a rural lawman gets a chance to nab the

killer of a national celebrity," Ralph said. "Andy will be big news when he arrests Sporn."

"He'll probably get offers from big city police departments, coast-to-coast," Sophie added.

"Including ours," Ike replied. "But I doubt that Andy would ever want to leave here. He's a great outdoorsman— loves hunting and fishing and country life in general."

"Besides that, Andy strikes me as modest," Liz said. "He might believe he wouldn't have cracked the case if it hadn't been for our help and that he wouldn't do well as a big city police officer."

"Sooner or later, he would have gotten around to examining that plant container very carefully," Ike said. "It's the only object we're confident Sporn handled. Maybe Andy would have decided to dust it on the faint chance some of the smoother stones might hold prints, and he'd have seen the leaves down in there, or maybe, like you did, Liz, he'd have thought of leaves falling off and Sporn picking them up. It was only a matter of time, but with the governor breathing down his neck, he wouldn't have had that time."

He paused, casting Liz a smile so warm that it kindled her heart. "Thanks to you, the governor's elite corps of hot-shot detectives won't get the credit for solving this case," he said.

The warmth stayed with her while they continued to watch coverage of the case. A bulletin came on, reporting the arrival of Buford's parents at the Stroutsboro airport.

"Mr. and Mrs. Doakes are in seclusion at a motel while arrangements are being made for the transportation of their son's body to Texas," the newscaster announced. "Meanwhile, in Buford's hometown of Gulch City, black banners drape street lamps and store fronts along Main Street. Businesses plan to close on the day of the funeral, scheduled for Wednesday. With fans swarming into town, both motels reported no vacancy until after the funeral."

After telling viewers to stay tuned for live coverage from Gulch City, the newscaster turned the program over to commercials.

They continued watching the coverage. When it became repetitive, Ike switched off the set.

"They won't have to rehash much longer," he said. "Soon there'll be late breaking bulletins about Sporn's arrest." He checked his watch. "Andy should be showing up pretty soon."

His phone sounded at that moment. Seconds after he picked up, he broke into a big smile, saying, "That's great, Andy."

Liz, Sophie, and Ralph exchanged pleased glances. This could only mean that the prints on the plant leaves matched those on the glass taken from Sporn's room.

"Good news?" Liz asked, as Ike hung up the phone.

"Right," he replied. "It's a match."

More jubilant hugs ensued. Ike held Liz in his arms a trifle longer than called for. "You're incredible," he whispered, giving her a quick kiss before resuming his detective mode. "Andy will be here as soon as he can. Since it's Sunday and the DA isn't in his office, Andy has to track him down."

Quick as the kiss was, she noticed the look in his eyes afterwards was unlike any she'd ever seen before.

The house phone range at that moment.

"I hope that's not the manager asking us why we're all up here in the penthouse when we've checked out," Sophie said.

"Andy cleared it with the manager," Ike replied, reaching to pick up. "This might be Kohner calling to say Sporn's attorney has arrived."

It was Kohner. Although his words were not audible, his strident tone crackled from the speaker.

Ike listened, then replied, "The sheriff's not here, but we expect him soon."

More crackling from Kohner. "Okay, I'll have him call Sporn's room as soon as he gets here," Ike said. He hung up the phone with a wry grin. "I was tempted to tell him Andy's conferring with the District Attorney."

"That would have given Kohner something to think about," Ralph said. "Is Sporn's attorney here?"

"Not yet. Kohner said he just phoned from his car. He'll be here in about ten minutes."

The attorney would have plenty of time to get Sporn's story before Andy returned, Liz thought.

"If this guy handles legal business for Kohner and Sporn, he's not a criminal defense attorney," Ralph said. "Is he bringing one with him?"

"Maybe Kohner thinks the case is so flimsy, there's no need for a defense attorney," Sophie said.

"Would an attorney skilled in criminal law be handling routine legal affairs?" Liz asked.

"It's possible," Ike replied. "He could be a former prosecutor now in private practice, or a former defense attorney who switched gears."

Whatever Sporn's attorney might be, he was up against a solid wall of evidence, Liz thought. From her many talks with Pop about police procedure, she knew what was likely to happen. If it could be determined that Sporn drowned Buford while in a blind rage, he'd be charged with voluntary manslaughter. Confronted with the undeniable physical evidence against his client, plus the highly incriminating circumstantial evidence, Sporn's attorney would go for a plea bargain.

Sophie's voice came into her thoughts. "I'm getting hungry. After Andy comes back, could we go down to the dining room for some dinner?"

Ralph laughed. "My ever-starving sweetheart! What do you think, Ike? Could we grab a meal after Andy comes back?"

"Sure," Ike replied. "I guess we'd all like to eat pretty soon. Just give Andy time to confer with Sporn's attorney. It shouldn't take long. Then the five of us will have dinner."

"A celebration dinner," Liz said. Now, still basking in the warmth of Ike's smile, and remembering the look in his eyes, she was struck with a heady feeling. Before this weekend was over, maybe she'd have more to celebrate than solving the case.

Chapter Twenty-three

Ike steered his Taurus out of Lorenzo's parking area and started up the hill. Glancing at Liz, he said, "This was a weekend none of us will ever forget. And the way you came up with the physical evidence—did I tell you you're incredible?"

"Yes, but you can tell me again," she replied. She almost added, "A woman can never hear her man say things like that too often," but despite that wonderful new look in his eyes, he had to make her believe he *was* her man, and she wanted the look translated into words before she took anything for granted. She'd already heard the three little words. Now it was time to hear the four.

The toot of a car horn sounded behind them. She turned and through the rear window waved to Sophie and Ralph in Gram's Chevy. When she and Sophie came here for the weekend, they could never have imagined they'd be driving home with Ike and Ralph, she thought. But, beyond any wild imaginings was the murder of Buford Doakes and their part in solving the case. She reviewed their discouraging search for the physical evidence and felt a surge of pride that she'd been the one who'd found it.

"I don't want to overdo telling you you're incredible," Ike said. "It might lose some of its impact."

While she was thinking *never*, he turned the radio on.

"Let's see if Sporn's arrest has hit the news yet," he said.

At dinner, Andy had filled them all in on his meeting with Attorney Harry Glick and Sporn, and the subsequent arrest, but Liz knew that hearing it broadcast would add extra satisfaction. When the news station came on, commercials were in progress. While waiting for them to end, she thought about what Andy had told them.

"I got the feeling Sporn wasn't quite with it," he'd said. "Strange, but he seemed almost relaxed during the meeting."

Relaxed and relieved, Liz thought, because he believed the threat to his marriage was over. He believed his wife would never know about his transgression. It was as if this was all that mattered.

"I can't help feeling sorry for Sporn," she said.

"Yeah, he's kind of pathetic," Ike agreed, turning the car onto the road that led to the highway. "I've never run across a killer like him."

Andy had told them that Sid Kohner had to be ejected, almost forcibly, from Sporn's room before the arrest. Liz felt a jot of compassion for Kohner, too. His golden goose was history, and the music arranger, whom he seemed to care about, faced a prison sentence.

But she had no such feelings for Sporn's wife. Although Sporn had brought this on himself, under her influence he'd become a foppish puppet. She'd pulled the strings that got him moving toward murder.

The news came on with the announcement of Sporn's arrest. This was followed by a bulletin. The governor had made a statement praising Sheriff Andy MacDuff for the speedy apprehension of Buford Doakes' killer.

"That's a big switch from before," Liz said. "I hope Andy hears about it."

"If he doesn't catch this broadcast, it'll be on again, all day," Ike replied.

Coverage of Sporn's arrest resumed. As Andy had told them earlier, Sporn was taken to Stroutsboro for booking and was jailed pending a hearing. The newscaster said that Attorney Glick had made no statement.

"Don't defense attorneys generally come out with statements saying their clients are innocent?" Liz asked.

"Right," Ike said, switching the radio off. "He must think the evidence in this case is overwhelming. You remember Andy told us Sporn appeared close to confessing to the drowning and to locking you and Sophie in the cave too."

"What next?" Liz asked.

"I expect Glick will advise Sporn to make a full confession in exchange for a plea bargain."

"Pop told me sentences are usually lighter with plea bargains. What do you think Sporn will get?"

"Depends on the judge. For voluntary manslaughter it could be five to fifteen—maybe more with the other charge."

He slowed the car as they approached the exit leading onto the route to Manhattan. While turning off, they waved good-bye to Staten Island-bound Sophie and Ralph.

"There are still some unanswered questions," Liz said. "Why did Sporn decide to follow Sophie and me on the trail? He didn't know we were gong to stumble on the cave and go inside so he could conveniently lock us in. Do you think because he believed we were detectives, he hoped to overhear some of our conversation and find out if he might be a suspect?"

"There's no telling what his reasoning was, but one thing's certain. When he saw you go into the cave, he acted on impulse. He didn't stop to think things through."

Liz nodded. This tied in with her own conclusions about Sporn's far-out mind. "Well, anyway, Andy got his man," she said. "Andy's a great guy. I like him a lot."

Ike cast her a quick look. "He likes you a lot, too."

"Our little group of sleuths put in plenty of time together. He got to like all of us."

"You, especially," Ike replied.

"How do you know that?"

"He told me so, and he asked me how things stood between you and me."

Liz's heart went into a spin. All she could manage to say was, "Oh?"

"Yeah, he said he noticed Sophie was wearing an engagement ring but you weren't, and he wanted to know if I had serious intentions about you."

She took a deep breath to calm herself. "And . . . and . . . what did you say?"

"I said damn right I did."

She was too dazed to reply. He glanced at her. She saw puzzlement in his eyes. "You knew that, didn't you, Liz?"

Still dazed, she shook her head. "I wasn't sure."

He slowed the car, pulled off onto the shoulder and braked. "I'm a first class idiot. I should have made you sure," he said, closing his arms around her.

After a lingering kiss, he smiled into her eyes. "Are you sure, now?"

Whatever words she might have said, he silenced her with a light kiss. "Don't answer that, answer *this*," he said. "If I show up at your place in a couple of days with a diamond ring, will you be sure, then?"

Her heart gave a joyful leap before settling into contented rhythm. The four words she wanted to hear were still unspoken, but it didn't matter anymore. Soon she'd have proof those words were in his heart. She'd have the physical evidence.

"Yes," she said.